P9-DNO-086

SPRINGDALE PUBLIC LIBRARY
405 S. Pleasant
Springdale, AR 72764

A FAIR MAIDEN

FAIR
MAIDEN

JOYCE CAROL OATES

AN OTTO PENZLER BOOK

HOUGHTON MIFFLIN HARCOURT
BOSTON   NEW YORK
2010

SPRINGDALE PUBLIC LIBRARY
405 S. Pleasant
Springdale, AR 72764

Copyright © 2010 by The Ontario Review, Inc.

ALL RIGHTS RESERVED

For information about permission to reproduce selections from this book,
write to Permissions, Houghton Mifflin Harcourt Publishing Company,
215 Park Avenue South, New York, New York 10003.

www.hmhbooks.com

Library of Congress Cataloging-in-Publication Data
Oates, Joyce Carol, date
A fair maiden / Joyce Carol Oates. — 1st ed.
p.   cm.
"An Otto Penzler Book."
ISBN 978-0-15-101516-0
1. Teenage girls — Fiction.   I. Title.
PS3565.A8F34 2009
813'.54 — dc22   2008029359

Book design by Brian Moore

Printed in the United States of America

DOC 10 9 8 7 6 5 4 3 2 1

for

Jeanne Wilmot Carter

So slowly, slowly, she came up
And slowly she came nigh him.
And all she said when there she came,
Young man, I think you're dying.

—*The Ballad of Barbara Allen*

PART I

1

INNOCENTLY IT BEGAN. When Katya Spivak was sixteen years old and Marcus Kidder was sixty-eight.

On Ocean Avenue of Bayhead Harbor, New Jersey, in the thickening torpor of late-morning heat she'd been pushing the Engelhardts' ten-month-old baby in his stroller and clutching the hand of the Engelhardts' three-year-old daughter, Tricia, passing the succession of dazzling and dreamlike shops for which Ocean Avenue was known — the Bridal Shoppe, the Bootery, the Wicker House, Ralph Lauren, Lily Pulitzer, Crowne Jewels, the Place Setting, Pandora's Gift Box, Prim Rose Lane Lingerie & Nightwear — when, as she paused to gaze into the Prim Rose Lane window, there came an unexpected voice in her ear: "And what would you choose, if you had your wish?"

What registered was the quaint usage *your wish. Your wish,* like something in a fairy tale.

At sixteen she was too old to believe in fairy tales, but she did believe in what might be promised by a genial male voice urging *your wish.*

With a smile she turned to him. In Bayhead Harbor, it was generally a good idea to lead with a smile. For possibly she knew this person, who'd been following her, keeping pace with her in the periphery of her vision, not passing her as other pedestrians did as she dawdled in front of store windows. In Bayhead Harbor, where everyone was so friendly, you naturally turned to even a stranger with a smile, and it was something of a disappointment to her to see that the stranger was an older, white-haired, gentlemanly man in a seersucker sport coat of the hue of ripe cantaloupe, white sport shirt and spotless white cord trousers, sporty white yachtsman's shoes. His eyes were a frank icy blue, crinkled at the corners from decades of smiling. Like a romantic figure in a Hollywood musical of bygone days — Fred Astaire? Gene Kelly? — he was even leaning on a carved ebony cane. "Well! I'm waiting, dear. What is your wish?"

In the Prim Rose Lane display window were such silky, intimate items of apparel, it seemed very strange that anyone who passed by could see them, and yet more unnerving that others might observe. Katya had been staring at a red lace camisole and matching red lace panties — silk, sexy, ridiculously expensive — worn by an elegantly thin blond mannequin with a bland beautiful face, but it was a white muslin Victorian-style nightgown with satin trim, on a girl mannequin with braids, to which she pointed. "That," Katya said.

"Ah! Impeccable taste. But you weren't looking at something else, were you? As I said, my dear, you have your choice."

My dear. Katya laughed uncertainly. No one spoke like this; on TV, in movies, maybe. *My dear* was meant to be quaint, and comical. *You are so young, and I am so old. If I acknowledge this with a joke, will I come out on top?*

He introduced himself as "Marcus Kidder, longtime Bayhead Harbor summer resident." This too sounded playful, as if Kidder had to be a joke. But his smile was so sincere, his manner so cordial, Katya saw no harm in volunteering her name, in abbreviated form: "I'm Katya. I'm a nanny." Pausing to suggest how silly, how demeaning the very term *nanny* was — she hated it. She was spending July and August until Labor Day working for a couple named Engelhardt, from Saddle River, New Jersey; the Engelhardts had just built a split-level house on New Liberty Street, on one of the harbor channels. "Maybe you know them? Max and Lorraine? They belong to the Bayhead Harbor Yacht Club."

"Doubtful that I do," Mr. Kidder said with a polite sneer. "If your employers are among the swarm of new people multiplying along the Jersey coast like mayflies."

Katya laughed. Dignified Mr. Kidder didn't like the Engelhardts any more than she did, and he didn't even know them.

Was he going to offer to buy her the nightgown? It seemed to have been forgotten, for which Katya was both grateful and mildly disappointed.

Though there was no doubt in her mind how she'd have reacted: *Mr. Kidder, no thanks!*

"Well, I have to leave now," Katya said, edging away. "Goodbye."

"And I, too. In this direction."

And so Mr. Kidder fell into step with Katya, walking with her on Ocean Avenue and making sparkly conversation with Tricia, a shy child, now a not-so-shy child, beguiled by this charming old white-haired man who, so far as a three-year-old could know, might be a grandfatherly friend or acquaintance of her parents'. Now in the succession of shop windows Katya was aware of two reflections — her own, and that of the tall, white-haired Mr. Kidder. You would think, *An attractive pair!* Katya smiled in the hope that passersby might imagine them together, maybe related. She was thinking how unusual it was to see a man of Mr. Kidder's age so tall, at least six feet two. And he carried himself with such dignity, his shoulders so straight. And his clothes — those were expensive clothes. And that striking white hair, soft-floating white, lifting in two wings from his high forehead. His skin was creased like a glove lightly crushed in the hand and was slightly recessed beneath the eyes, yet no more, Katya thought, than her own bruised-looking eyes when she had to push herself out of bed at an early hour after an insomniac night. Mr. Kidder's face was flushed with color, however, as if blood pulsed warmly just below the surface of his skin. He appeared to be of an age far beyond that of Katya's father, yet she couldn't believe that he was her grandfather's age: that terrifying limbo of free fall when specific ages become, to the young, beside the point. To the young there are no meaningful degrees of *old*, as there are no degrees of *dead*: either you are, or you are not.

Katya noticed that Mr. Kidder winced just slightly, walking with his cane. Yet he meant to be entertaining, telling her and Tricia that he had a "new, one-hundred-percent nonorganic plastic" right knee: "Have you ever heard of anything so amazing?"

Katya said, "Sure we have. People can buy new knees — hips — hearts — lungs — if they have the money. Nothing needs to wear out, if you're rich. Tricia here will live to be one hundred and ten. Her parents expect it."

Katya laughed, and Mr. Kidder joined in. Exactly why, neither could have said.

"And what of you, dear Katya? How long do you expect to live?"

"Me? Not long at all. Maybe until I'm . . . forty. That's old enough." Carelessly Katya spoke, with a shiver of distaste. Her mother was over forty. Katya had no wish to resemble *her*.

"Forty is far too young, dear Katya!" Mr. Kidder protested. "Why do you say such a thing?"

He seemed genuinely surprised, disapproving. Katya felt the warmth of his disapproval, which was so very different from the chill disapproval of her family. *Katya has a mouth on her! A mouth that wants slapping.*

"Because I have bad habits."

"Bad habits! I can scarcely believe that." Mr. Kidder frowned, intrigued.

Why she sometimes spoke as she did, Katya didn't know. *The mouth speaks what the ear is to hear.*

Wanting to impress this man, maybe. Flattered by his interest in her, though she guessed she knew what it was, or might be; yet somehow she didn't think that was it. Older men often looked at her — Mr. Engelhardt often gazed at her with a small, distracted

[6]

smile — but that was different somehow. Katya could not have said why, but she knew.

Now they were passing the large, lavish display window of Hilbreth Home Furnishings, and Mr. Kidder touched Katya's wrist lightly. "And in this window, Katya, what would you choose, for your dream home?"

Dream home. Another quaint usage that stirred Katya's pulse.

The first time she'd looked into Hilbreth's window, Katya had felt something sharp turn in her heart: a stab of dismay, resentment, dislike, anger against those who bought such expensive things for their expensive homes, and a childish envy. Yet now, at Mr. Kidder's playful urging, she gazed into the window with a small smile of anticipation. Such elegantly spare, angular furniture! Here there were no comfortably cushioned sofas or chairs, no bright chintz or floral patterns, scarcely any colors. Instead there was a preponderance of chrome, there was sleek black leather, low tables of sculpted wood, heavy slabs of tinted glass. Wheat-colored cushions in profusion, flat dull rugs, gigantic table lamps and skeletal floor lamps that didn't seem to require light bulbs . . . In Vineland, New Jersey, which was Katya's home town, inland in the scrubby Pine Barrens, you would not encounter objects remotely like these, just soft, formless, graceless things, soiled and sagging sofas, worn vinyl chairs, Formica-topped tables.

"Anything from this window," Katya said, smiling so that her words wouldn't be misinterpreted as sarcastic, "I would need a special house for."

With an ambiguous smile of his own, Mr. Kidder said, "Maybe that could be arranged."

Katya shivered. Though Mr. Kidder was joking, of course, in the dazzling display window her reflection shimmered like a fairy figure in water.

Mr. Kidder had not inquired where Katya was taking the children, and Katya had not volunteered the information. Yet he expressed no surprise when Katya crossed Chapel Street, and now Post Road, when Katya pushed the stroller into Harbor Park. Here Tricia would feed the noisy waterfowl for twenty minutes or so and, if circumstances were right, mingle with other children in the park. Here were a half-dozen swans, many fat waddling Canada geese, platoons of smaller geese and mallards wriggling their feathered bottoms as they rushed forward to be fed. Tricia delighted in tossing bread bits to the waterfowl, which was, like their daily outings to the beach, a high point of her day. Katya had quickly come to dislike "feeding the geese," which seemed to provoke hunger more than satisfy it and made the birds contend with one another in a way that was crudely comical, too pointedly human. In Harbor Park much of the grass near the lake had been dirtied by the birds' myriad droppings; the lake was really no more than a large pond, shrunken in midsummer. Other nannies — most of them Hispanic, and older than Katya — brought small Caucasian children to the park to toss bits of bread at the clamorous birds; Katya had begun to recognize some of these women. As if she'd been trekking to Harbor Park for months, not less than two weeks.

Katya provided Tricia with bread for the birds and cautioned her not to get too close to them. As Tricia ran off excitedly, Mr. Kidder, looking after her, said, "You wish, don't you, that they would always stay that age . . ." He spoke sentimentally, leaning on his cane.

Katya said, "No. I hated being so small, and I hated being so weak. It was scary — adults are so *tall*."

"And now we're not so tall to you?"

"Yes. Those of you who matter. And I'm still afraid of you."

"Afraid of *me*, dear Katya? Surely not."

Katya laughed. If this was a flirtation — and it felt like a flirtation — it was like no other flirtation in Katya's experience: with a man old enough to be her grandfather? (Though in fact very different from Katya's grandfather Spivak, stooped and tremulous

[8]

from a lifetime of heavy drinking.) Meaning to shock him mildly, she said, "Know what I'd like right now? A cigarette."

"A cigarette! Not from me."

She'd begun smoking when she was twelve. One of Katya's bad habits.

In middle school she'd begun. If you were a girl and good-looking, older boys provided you with cigarettes as with other contraband: joints, uppers, beer. Katya would not have smoked in the Engelhardt children's presence, of course. She would not have dared to smoke in any circumstances in which her employers might observe her, or in which she might be reported back to her employers, for at their interview Mrs. Engelhardt had asked if she smoked and Katya had assured her no. And she didn't drink. ("Why, I should hope not" — Mrs. Engelhardt's prim response.)

In a wistful tone, Mr. Kidder was saying that he'd smoked for many years — "Deplorable, delicious habit, like all habits that endanger us." He smiled, as if he had more to say on this intriguing subject but had thought better of it. "But, dear Katya! It pains me to think of you smoking so young. Such an attractive girl, so healthy-seeming, with all your young life before you . . ."

Katya shrugged. "That's why, maybe. That long way ahead."

Again Katya felt that she'd shocked this man, unsettled him. Their conversation, which appeared to be so wayward, casual, haphazard and spontaneous, like the children's cries as they tossed bread to the waterfowl, was more accurately following a deeper, more deliberate route, like an underground stream that, from the surface of the ground, you can't detect. All this while Katya was gently jiggling the stroller in which the baby was strapped, a mindless rhythmic action that made the baby smile moistly up at her, as if with love. Easy to mistake for love, Katya thought.

In Vineland, Katya frequently looked after small children, including her older sister's children, and she had come to the conclusion that she wanted no children of her own, not ever. But here in Bayhead Harbor, where the children of summer residents were so prized, and exuded an unexpected glamour, she had to reconsider.

"How old are you, my dear? If you don't mind my asking."

How old are you? Katya bit her lower lip with a sly smile but said instead, "How old do I look?"

In her T-shirt and denim cutoffs, with her smooth, tanned bare legs and arms, streaked-blond ponytail, and calm, steely gray eyes lifted provocatively to Mr. Kidder's face, Katya knew that she looked good. She was five feet five inches tall, slender but not thin, the calves of her legs taut, hard. Mr. Kidder's eyes moved over her with appreciation. "I assume you must be at least . . . sixteen? To be trusted as a nanny? Though you look younger, in fact."

"Your granddaughter's age?"

Mr. Kidder's smile tightened. Curtly he said, "I don't have a granddaughter. That is, not a blood relation."

Katya felt the sting of a rebuke. The icy blue eyes, tight fixed smile. With the tip of his cane Mr. Kidder had been tracing invisible patterns in the ground at his feet.

"Kidder. Is that a real name, or just something you made up?"

"Kidder is certainly real. Marcus Kidder is painfully real. Let me give you my card, dear Katya." Out of his wallet Mr. Kidder drew a small white printed card, and on the back of the card he scribbled his unlisted — "magic" — number.

Marcus Cullen Kidder
17 Proxmire Street
Bayhead Harbor, N.J.

"Come see me someday soon, Katya. Bring little Tricia and her delightful baby brother — if you wish. Tomorrow, tea-time?"

Katya slipped the little white card into a pocket. "Yes. Maybe." Coolly thinking, *I don't think so.*

Just then the waterfowl erupted. One of the children had tossed down a large chunk of bread, provoking a skirmish among the excited birds: flapping wings, agitated squawks, an angry confrontation between Canada geese and the more audacious of the mallards. "Tricia! Come here." Katya ran to lift the frightened little girl into her arms as she began to cry. "Sweetie, you aren't hurt. These are just noisy birds. They get hungry, and they get excited. We'll leave now." Katya felt a stab of guilt, that she'd been distracted by talking with Mr. Kidder: what if one of the larger birds had pecked at Tricia's bare legs — worse yet, her arms, her face . . .

"Shoo! Shoo!" Mr. Kidder waved at the birds with his cane, scattering them and sending them back to the water. Like a comical yet gallant figure in a children's movie, a protector of the young. He meant to be amusing, to make the frightened children laugh, and their nannies. But Katya did not laugh.

"Tricia, come on. Let's go back to the house."

She'd had enough of the park, and she'd had enough of her white-haired gentleman friend. She'd had enough of Katya Spivak preening for his benefit and felt a wave of revulsion and dread, that she'd made a mistake in spending so much time with him and in having taken his card. As she hurried away with the Engelhardt children, Mr. Kidder called urgently after her, offering to summon a taxi for them or, if they walked over to his house — "Close by, a five-minute walk" — to drive them back himself. But Katya called over her shoulder, "No! No thanks! That isn't a good idea right now."

My darling, I thought then that I had lost you. Before I even knew you.

2

"A ROLL OF THE DICE. Let the dice decide."

Smiling, recalling her father's words from long ago. When she'd been a little girl who'd adored her daddy, not knowing how her daddy was a compulsive gambler, which was a bad habit in the Spivak family only when you lost big. So long as Jude Spivak's losses were reasonably small, only just interspersed with wins, maybe gambling wasn't a bad habit at all.

As Katya remembered, her mother had liked it just fine when Katya's daddy had won. No furious condemnations of "compulsive gambling" so long as he brought money home. In fact, hugs and kisses. In fact, celebrating by getting drunk.

Let the dice decide was a cool way of saying *Take a chance, see what happens, why the hell not?*

Not a good idea, maybe! But Katya was going to execute it.

He was an elderly man, with an eye for her. He was a rich man, and he was (shrewdly, she knew) a lonely man. In Atlantic City, such men were *marks*. Such men were asking to be *exploited, duped.*

She would return to him. Quite deliberately — consciously — shrewdly she would return to Mr. Kidder in that mansion of his.

Not the day after they'd met — that would be too soon. Let him wait a while, and worry that pretty blond sixteen-year-old Katya wasn't coming back.

Nor the day following, either (an exhausting day spent on Mr. Engelhardt's showy thirty-foot Chris-Craft powerboat bucking the waves to Cape May and back — an "outing" providing as much pleasure for the harassed nanny as being taken for a jarring ride on a lawn mower across corrugated ground). Next day was a Monday — by which day Katya reckoned that Mr. Kidder would have given up expecting visitors.

Just a roll of the dice. She was risking nothing. No danger in upscale Bayhead Harbor, which was very different from Atlantic City, fifty miles to the south, where Katya Spivak would never have been so naive as to go to a man's house, no matter how harmless he appeared, how gentlemanly or how rich.

Of course, she wasn't going alone: she wasn't that naive. She would take little Tricia with her, and the baby in his stroller. Not really risky by Spivak family standards.

So on Monday, after they'd fed the noisy waterfowl in the park, as if she'd just thought of it, Katya squatted before three-year-old Tricia and asked if she'd like to visit that "nice funny old white-haired man with the cane, who was so friendly the other day," and predictably Tricia cried *Yes!*, and so Katya saw no harm in taking Tricia and Tricia's little brother in his stroller to Mr. Kidder's house a few blocks away.

If Mrs. Engelhardt found out and asked about the visit, Katya might say that Tricia had wanted to return, Tricia had *insisted*. She could not have reasonably argued that 17 Proxmire Street was on her way back to the Engelhardts' house on New Liberty Street. For Mr. Kidder lived in the much-revered "historic" — "landmark" — section of Bayhead Harbor, near picturesque Bayhead Lighthouse and the open ocean. As the open ocean was very different from the narrow boat channels in the Engelhardts' newly developed neighborhood, so the air nearer the ocean was distinctly cooler and fresher and smelled bracingly of water, sand, sun.

Money too, Katya thought. *A special kind of money-smell*, which had nothing to do with grubby paper bills you might actually hold in your hand and count. Nothing to do with coins sweating in the palm of a hand. This was money that was invisible, the money of true wealth.

The Engelhardts and their friends spoke enviously of these older, spacious oceanfront properties that so rarely came on the market or, if they did, sold overnight for several million dollars. Katya felt a stab of satisfaction; the Engelhardts would envy *her*, a visitor in Mr. Kidder's house.

I am special. Mr. Kidder wants me.

She laughed, this was so delicious. She was feeling very good.

On Proxmire Street, pushing the baby's stroller and staring at the enormous houses. And not just the houses — "properties," as they were called — several times the size of the crowded lots in the Engelhardts' neighborhood of showy split-levels and A-frames. And the stately ten-foot privet hedges that shielded the houses here from the street and the curious stares of sightseers hoping to gaze at the homes of the wealthy as you might gaze into the dazzling shop windows of Ocean Avenue.

Katya liked it that the house at 17 Proxmire was old and dignified and weathered — a "shingleboard" house — with white shutters, winking lattice windows, and a steep slate roof like an illustration in a children's storybook of a tale set *once upon a time.*

There was an entrance in the privet hedge. And a wonderful old wrought-iron gate, shut but not locked.

No solicitors.

All deliveries to the rear.

Katya laughed. These admonitions did not apply to *her.*

"Well, Tricia! Here we are — Mr. Kidder's house."

Her heart beat in anticipation of an adventure. Katya was a girl who craved adventure. How bored she was here in Bayhead Harbor, playing the role of nanny to people she hated. Two weeks! That was more than enough.

Thinking reasonably, *If the old man isn't home, go away. Never try again.*

Katya pushed the stroller along the surprisingly uneven flagstone walk to the front door, as Tricia walked shyly beside her. Were both feeling that Mr. Kidder might be watching them from one of the latticed windows, invisible behind the glittering glass? Like a scene in a movie, this seemed to Katya; she felt the man's eyes on her . . . Yet she was hearing a piano being played inside the house, which didn't sound like a radio or a recording.

On the wide front flagstone step Katya dared to ring the doorbell. When Tricia began to speak, Katya put a forefinger to her lips: "Shhh!"

There was a sort of magic here. Katya felt it. She could not behave carelessly, or let the child prattle. They were both very excited.

Whoever was inside had not heard the bell, it seemed. Katya tried again, and this time the piano-playing ceased and a few seconds later the heavy oak door swung open, inward — and there stood Mr. Kidder, blinking and staring at them as if, for a moment, he didn't know who they were.

"Why, it's — Katie? I mean — Katya. My dear, you've come . . ."

Mr. Kidder was smiling strangely, not welcoming her exactly, a wary sort of smile, dazed and wary and not what she'd expected. And he'd almost forgotten her name! Katya's face smarted with hurt. Well, he had not forgotten *her,* at least.

The greeting was very awkward. Katya thought, *Damn — this is a mistake.* But she could not back away. Of course she could not back away. Nervously she laughed — there was an edge of cruelty in her laughter — for Mr. Kidder was startled to see her, and nervous; his blue eyes were not so composed now, and not so icy; in his face was a sick-sinking expression of something like abject and raw desire he hoped to disguise, as a starving dog might try to hide his terrible ravenous appetite.

"Can't stay long, Mr. Kidder! We were just walking home from the park and Tricia said . . ."

Mr. Kidder was fumbling to tuck his loose shirt into his baggy shorts, which were wrinkled; clumsily he made a gesture as if to smooth down his fluffy white hair, which looked as if it hadn't been combed yet that day. "You've taken me by surprise, dear

Katya — but what a lovely surprise — and dear Tricia — and Tricia's baby brother, whose name is —"

Tricia giggled, providing her little brother's name as if this were a fact of supreme importance: "Kevin."

"Why of course — Kevin. How could I have forgotten!"

Where was the playful dignified gentleman of the other day, who had so impressed Katya? In khaki shorts worn without a belt, in a wrinkled white cotton shirt with short silly boxy sleeves, and with sandals on his bony pale feet, Mr. Kidder could have been any older man at whom a sixteen-year-old girl wouldn't have so much as glanced. Accustomed to dark-tanned men and boys in Bayhead Harbor, as in Vineland, Katya saw with particular distaste Mr. Kidder's naked feet and thin legs, lacking in muscle and near hairless.

Quickly Mr. Kidder said, "Come in! Come in. In fact, I was eagerly awaiting you — the trio of you."

"Were you!" Katya laughed, just subtly sneering.

"I was. Indeed I was. 'Tickling the ivories' — playing piano to evoke a lyric mood. In fact" — repeating *in fact* as if he were trying to cast a spell on Katya, who continued to stare at him — "it was my magical piano-playing, the first dreamy movement of Beethoven's 'Moonlight Sonata,' that drew the trio of you here."

Katya laughed, this was so fanciful. Very likely Tricia would believe what Mr. Kidder was telling them.

"You are just in time, my dears. Katya, do come *in*. For everyone else in my life seems to be *gone*."

"Gone? Where?"

"Oh, nowhere! Everywhere. Wherever people disperse to, like milkweed fluff, when they *go*."

Katya wasn't sure that she liked this. Gone? Everyone?

Gaily Mr. Kidder ushered them into the house. Firmly Mr. Kidder shut the door.

A heavy oak door. Katya wondered if it automatically locked, inside.

As Mr. Kidder chattered, a flush rising into his cheeks, Katya smiled uncertainly, gripping Tricia by the hand. Maybe this was a mistake and she was putting these helpless young children at risk . . . With a flurry of his hands, as if to dispel such ridiculous thoughts, Mr. Kidder said, "My fickle houseguests have departed for the city just this morning, you see. Not that I wanted them to stay, nooo! For I knew that Katya, Tricia, and Kevin were imminent. And so the house looms large and empty as a — we will not say *mausoleum*. No, no! We *will not*. And Mrs. Bee — dear Mrs. Bee — has Mondays off and has quite *buzzed away*."

Houseguests? Mrs. Bee? Katya knew what *mausoleum* meant and hoped that Tricia wouldn't repeat the word later that day, as children of her age sometimes did, like parrots. So far as she could see from the foyer, the enormous house did appear to be empty: rooms opening onto rooms, hallways leading into hallways, as in a maze of mirrors infinitely reflecting. "I had not expected visitors this afternoon," Mr. Kidder said somberly, "though last night there was a moon, and this moon peeked into my bedroom window and said, 'Whatever you do, M.K.' — for, from the lunar perspective, we are no more than our initials — 'do not eat up all those delicious strawberries in the refrigerator,' and I asked why, and the moon winked and said, 'You will see, M.K.' And now my special visitors have arrived, I see."

This spirited little speech was delivered for Tricia's benefit, but it was Katya for whom Mr. Kidder was performing, she thought. By quick degrees he was becoming increasingly confident, like an actor now recalling lines and no longer flailing about, blinded by the spotlight.

"This way! We will have tea on the terrace."

The first thing you saw, stepping into the living room of Mr. Kidder's house, was the far wall, entirely glass, overlooking the ocean in the near distance. For at this elevation on Proxmire Street you couldn't see the beach; if anyone was on the beach below, you couldn't see them; you saw only dunes, dune grass, the choppy ocean, the distant horizon. You saw the sky, which was a faint, misty blue, and a sickle moon just visible by daylight.

Katya felt something turn in her heart: a stab of hurt, envy. "This is so beautiful, Mr. . . ." She seemed to have forgotten Mr. Kidder's name. She could not help it that the flat nasal accent of south Jersey had an accusing tone even when meant to be admiring.

Graciously Mr. Kidder said that beauty is a matter of "seeing" — "seeing with fresh eyes, with the eyes of youth." So long he'd been spending summers at the Jersey shore in this house, as a child, as an adult, from June through Labor Day, he no longer saw what was.

He led them outside, onto a flagstone terrace. Here it was windy, much cooler than it had been on the street. And here even more beautiful: the view of the dunes, the rolling white-capped waves.

At the Bayhead Harbor Yacht Club beach there were usually so many other people around, Katya was distracted. Now she settled Tricia into a chair and saw that baby Kevin was comfortable sucking on his pacifier. She'd have to inform Mrs. Engelhardt of this visit, she supposed, since Tricia, who chattered about the least little thing encountered on their outings, would surely tell her. Shrewdly, Katya thought there might be a way — she would find a way — to suggest that there'd been other guests at Mr. Kidder's "tea-time," Mr. Kidder's housekeeper at least.

Katya helped Mr. Kidder bring things out to the terrace, for the white-haired man was obviously unaccustomed to such practical tasks as setting a table and serving food. Katya took from Mr. Kidder's uncertain hand a heavy cut-glass pitcher of lemonade, and deftly she spooned strawberries and sherbet into shallow cut-glass bowls. Out of a baker's box she took vanilla wafers and arranged them on a plate. She was amused to see that while Mr. Kidder had been out of her sight he'd tucked his shirt more firmly into the baggy khaki shorts and he'd tried to tamp down his unruly hair. And possibly he'd taken a quick sip of something that smelled sweetly tart on his breath, like red wine.

Mr. Kidder sat at the head of a heavy white wrought-iron table, beaming at his guests. "I'd about given up, you know. I'd begun to think that our little Tricia preferred those noisy old geese with their messy ways to Marcus Kidder."

Their tea-time passed in this way, Mr. Kidder addressing Tricia or the baby, all the while glancing sidelong at Katya, as if there were an intimate rapport between them that didn't require overt acknowledgment. Katya considered asking him for a glass of wine. No doubt he'd have been disapproving. Yet intrigued. Katya was what the law calls a minor — it was a felony in New Jersey to serve liquor to a minor, even unknowingly. How strange it was to be sitting close beside this stranger, at an elegant wrought-iron table that must have weighed a hundred pounds, on chairs so heavy Katya could scarcely budge them; strange, and not strange, that their knees should touch beneath the table, accidentally.

This was quite the most exciting event of Katya Spivak's summer, so far. She was feeling a thrill of pride, a wave of childlike happiness, that she was here: at this table, on this terrace at 17 Proxmire Street, overlooking the open ocean; she, whose father had been a part-owner of a garage in Vineland, with his brothers, before he'd lost his share of the property and disappeared. Katya Spivak in "historic" Bayhead Harbor, being treated so politely, so graciously, by a rich old white-haired man named Kidder.

She would have liked to tell her mother, her older sisters, her brothers, and her cousins, who would envy her.

Boys she knew. One or two older boys, in Vineland.

This house! You would not believe. On the ocean, worth millions of dollars, the owner has to be a millionaire . . .

"And what are you thinking about, dear Katya? You seem to have drifted off."

In the wind Mr. Kidder's hair looked as if it were being roughly caressed by agitated hands. The wind was taking their breath away. Katya said she was thinking she'd like a glass of wine. If Mr. Kidder had wine . . . Seeing his startled expression, Katya laughed.

"I'm afraid — no. I don't have any wine. And if I did, my dear, I wouldn't be so reckless as to give some to *you*."

Meaning, *You are underage. You are off-limits.*

The wind! Tricia squealed as her napkin went fluttering and flying across the terrace like a live thing, and Katya jumped up to retrieve it. She saw Mr. Kidder's eyes trail over her tanned legs, the curve of her hips in the denim cutoffs. Thin streaks of cloud passed over the sun; there was a mild chill. Mr. Kidder said apologetically, "We should move inside, I think! It's one of those capricious days. Warm — now not so warm. And I have presents for you, dear Tricia and dear Katya, I dare not forget."

Presents! Tricia was thrilled. Katya smiled guardedly.

"Yes, we should go inside," Katya said. "We should be leaving soon, I think. Mrs. Engelhardt will be expecting us back . . ."

Was this true? Often when Katya returned to the split-level house on the channel, Mrs. Engelhardt's SUV was gone and only the Hispanic housekeeper was there.

Katya helped Mr. Kidder carry the tea things back into the house, into the largest kitchen she'd ever seen. He led her then into a room that was a kind of studio, overlooking the terrace from another angle, with lattice windows, floor-to-ceiling bookshelves, a sofa covered in brightly colored upholstery. The room smelled of paint and turpentine; in a corner was an easel, and on the floor a paint-splattered tarpaulin; against a wall, stacks of unframed canvases. On the walls were works of art — paintings, pastel drawings — portraits of women, girls, young children. So Mr. Kidder was an artist! When Katya complimented him on his work, which was impressive to her, with a smile he asked if she'd like to pose for him sometime.

"Pose? Like for a . . . portrait?"

"Depending on the results, portraits."

[20]

Meaning more than one? Katya was made to feel confused, uncertain. Those icy blue eyes were fixed upon her so intently. "When would I have time, Mr. Kidder? You know that I'm a nanny — my work hours are dawn to dusk."

She meant to be funny. Though what she said was true, essentially. She had two half-days off, Wednesday, Sunday, and even after dusk, after feeding the Engelhardt children, bathing them, and preparing them for bed, she felt, in a far corner of the house with no view of the channel, that she was expected to remain on duty.

"What about dusk, then? Night?"

Katya laughed uneasily, supposing that Mr. Kidder must be joking and not knowing how to reply.

While Mr. Kidder turned to Tricia, Katya drifted about the studio. So much to look at! She liked it that Mr. Kidder's furniture did not resemble the stark angular sculpted things in Hilbreth Home Furnishings, and she liked it that there were so many books on the shelves (books were a comfort to her), so many small carvings, vases and urns, glass flowers. Light struck and illuminated these flowers like flame.

Mr. Kidder was presenting Tricia with a gift: a children's picture book titled *Funny Bunny's Birthday Party*, with which Tricia was delighted. Katya glanced about, still uneasy: was there a present for her?

There didn't seem to be. Mr. Kidder was absorbed in Tricia, turning pages of the book for her, reading aloud. Katya stared at the glass flowers. She'd never seen anything like these flowers before. None seemed to resemble real flowers, or at least flowers familiar to her; their stalks and leaves were varying degrees of green, but their petals were the most exquisite colors, flaming crimson, iridescent purple, gold-striped, grotesquely shaped. There were petals that resembled tentacles and petals that resembled nerve filaments. Stamens that resembled tongues, pistils like eyes. Katya stared at a large flesh-colored peonylike flower that mimicked a seashell, or — she didn't want to think — the smooth hairless vagina of a young girl. With a nervous laugh, she asked, "Who made these, Mr. Kidder?" and Mr. Kidder solemnly bowed, with a sad-clown smirk: "M.K. — in a lyric phase of long ago. My 'fossil flowers.'"

Katya asked what a fossil flower was, and Mr. Kidder said that they were glass replicas of "long-extinct flowers" he'd become interested in as a young man. He got to his feet and came to stand beside Katya — close beside her. "Some of these will look familiar to you — they resemble flowers living today. These orchids, for instance. And this is an early ancestor of rose pogonia." The glass flowers were displayed in clusters, in vases; they were scattered through the room, and there were more than Katya had originally thought. She asked Mr. Kidder how glass could be sculpted — wouldn't it break? And Mr. Kidder smiled at her as if she'd said something clever. "Not in its molten state, Katya. Before we are sculpted, we are pliable raw material." She'd asked a stupid question, Katya understood. Of course, she knew that glass was "molten" — liquid.

In her embarrassment she pretended to be examining a bizarrely shaped flower with fat, sawtoothed petals, very sharp to the touch, and winced when she saw that she'd actually cut herself, a fine, near-invisible wound like a paper cut, which she managed to hide from Mr. Kidder. She was noticing that many of the fossil flowers, beautiful at a short distance, were finely cracked and covered in a thin film of dust. Not what you'd call dirty, not grimy, but not clean either. Such fragile things weren't practical. Living with them at close quarters, day after day, you couldn't keep them up; finally you'd resent them. Not even Mr. Kidder's housekeeper, Mrs. Bee, could keep his fossil flowers clean.

Mr. Kidder seemed just to have made this discovery, too. He'd wet his forefinger and was wiping at petals, frowning. "Beautiful useless things! I've ruined my life with them, who knows why. I was married once — in fact, I was married twice — to beauties. Beauty is my folly, and why? Freud said, 'Beauty has no discernible use. Yet without it, life would be unbearable.'"

Katya sucked surreptitiously at her finger, where the thin cut oozed a thin sliver of blood. Mr. Kidder took no notice. Mr. Kidder was brooding over the glass flowers and had spoken with unexpected feeling, almost bitterly. Katya didn't want their comical/dignified host to be suddenly serious, or sad. She said, to cheer the old man up, "Mr. Kidder, there isn't a thing in those stores on Ocean Avenue anything like these flowers. If I could make anything so beautiful ever in my life, I'd be so happy. I would never be unhappy or depressed again."

Mr. Kidder was smiling at her indulgently, with bemused eyes. "You, Katya, depressed, unhappy — my dear, that's hard to believe."

Katya laughed and shrugged. She was a hired girl; she said such things on order. Much of her life was this sort of semiskilled playing to other people, usually older people, with the hope of making them like her; making them feel that she was valuable to them; wresting some of their power from them, if but fleetingly. It was like provoking a boy or a man to want you. That could be risky, as Katya well knew. Katya thought, *He will give me one of the fossil flowers — that will be my reward.*

But Mr. Kidder seemed preoccupied and did not offer Katya one of the fossil flowers. She was disappointed, and she was hurt. Suddenly she wanted to be gone from 17 Proxmire Street.

The baby had wakened from his light doze and began to fret. No doubt his diaper was soaked. Katya must get him home quickly and change his diaper. "Goodbye, Mr. Kidder! Thank you for having us for tea-time."

"Katya, dear! Wait." Mr. Kidder roused himself to protest as Katya gathered up Tricia and adjusted the baby in his stroller. "I have something for you." But then he couldn't seem to find it, opening drawers, rummaging about on a shelf, sucking at his lips in old-man agitation. And then a tinsel-wrapped package was thrust into Katya's hands: a pink box from Prim Rose Lane Lingerie & Nightwear. Katya opened the package and saw inside not the little-girl white muslin nightgown but the sexy red lace camisole and matching red lace panties.

Katya's cheeks smarted as if she'd been slapped. Quickly she hid the red silk inside the tissue paper and shut the box up.

"I can't take this, Mr. Kidder. Thank you, but no."

She held out the box to him. She was upset, and she was angry. Mr. Kidder professed surprise and refused to take the box from her. "Don't be silly, Katya. Why can't you take this? It's really very attractive and very finely made and there is nothing wrong with accepting it from me. You know, you don't need to tell anyone about it."

"I don't want it. I don't wear things like this. I don't — want it." She was laughing, this was so absurd. An old man like Marcus Kidder, giving such lingerie to *her*. She fumbled for Tricia's hand and roused the little girl from *Funny Bunny's Birthday Party*, pushed the stroller toward the front door as Mr. Kidder accompanied her, apologizing. Yet you couldn't know if Mr. Kidder was truly apologetic or if he was teasing; if he was genuinely sorry he'd embarrassed and upset her or if he was laughing at her.

"Dear Katya! I never meant whatever it is you seem to think that I meant. And you can return the gift to the store — the receipt is inside."

Mr. Kidder followed Katya outside. At the privet-hedge entrance he extended his hand to her, gravely, but Katya would not take it. Both she and Mr. Kidder were breathing quickly. A hot flush had come into Katya's face. She was determined never to see Marcus Kidder again, never to return to this house. Above, the sky was layered in clouds thin as steam, obscuring the sun. The pale sickle moon had vanished. Katya was sure that she hadn't been in Mr. Kidder's house for even an hour, yet it felt much later.

Mr. Kidder continued to apologize, yet there appeared to be merriment in his eyes, not repentance. You could see that Marcus Kidder was a terrible tease; you could not trust Marcus Kidder. His behavior made little girls like Tricia laugh in delight as if they were being tickled. Tricia adored funny Mr. Kidder and shook hands goodbye, but Katya refused to shake his hand, Katya was grievously wounded in her soul. To her he said, "Come back another time, dear. When you are not so agitated. When you can come alone. And can stay longer. Your present will be awaiting you."

How furious you were, my darling! Yet you knew I did not mean to hurt you. And you knew, as I certainly did, that you'd be back.

3

"FUCK YOU, OLD MAN. You don't know *me*."

She was a blunt girl. She was a crude girl. She was an angry girl. For all the Spivaks were angry, and she was a Spivak. Yet she was a girl easily embarrassed, shamed. Many times a day she felt, like the fleeting shadows of clouds passing the sun, the kick in the gut *Shame! shame!*, all the while her mouth fixed in that faint half-smile: *Yes, I am a nice girl, I am a friendly and helpful girl, tell me what to do, give me instructions and I will do it.*

Minimum-wage jobs part-time, after school, and summers she'd been working since the age of thirteen, knowing she couldn't expect her parents to help pay for her college expenses even at the community college. Hospital bills, credit card debts — she'd ceased hearing. Her father's gambling debts: these had to be repaid. Or maybe the interest on the loans. Which was why she'd become a very capable girl. Not skinny, not weak like girls she saw here in Bayhead Harbor, rich girls she despised. Except if one of them, visiting the Engelhardts with her parents, smiled at Katya, asked where Katya was from, Katya's heart melted every time. For she was a girl who admired, adored, yearned to love many people. Though she hated many people! In school, since grade school, the friends she'd yearned for took little interest in her: she was a Spivak, and the Spivaks had acquired a certain reputation in Cumberland County, New Jersey. She was not a beautiful girl. She was a girl for boys to have sex with, except she would not have sex with them, which angered them. She was a shy girl; she distrusted her body. She did not see herself in a mirror and think, *That is me*, but she would think, *Is that me?*, staring in doubt, distrust. Nor did she trust her teachers when they praised her, encouraged her. You had to suspect that you were being pitied, if you were a Spivak. You had to suspect something. *They want to make you hopeful, and then they will laugh at you.* This was the sort of advice her mother might have given her. And her father, a different kind of advice: *Roll the dice, see what happens. Why the hell not?* There was logic here. Katya could appreciate the logic here. Still, she knew that her mother was right. She was not a girl likely to go to college except at the community college, and maybe not even there. She knew she had to prepare herself.

Since thirteen, she'd been preparing. She wasn't beautiful like these Bayhead Harbor girls, but it was surprising how men sometimes looked at her. More it was older men rather than guys her age, for some reason. For she was uneasy in her body. That fleshy lower lip, a sullen-sulky look on her face, which she wasn't aware of until her mother pointed it out. *That look of Katya's — makes you want to slap it off her face.* And that mouth of Katya's. She was mortified by such revelations. She was mortified by her body. *Tits, boobs, ass,* were ugly words that were mortifying to her, shameful. In sixth grade this had begun, hearing such words. And it would continue for the rest of her life, she believed. A female is her body. A guy can be lots of things, not just his body. She did not like guys to touch her. She did not like guys to kiss her and force their tongues in her mouth; this was disgusting to her. Why this was exciting and arousing to other girls, she could not imagine. A guy's tongue in her mouth made her want to gag, vomit. And worse than that in her mouth, she could not bear to consider. Though when she'd been high, and drunk, partying with her friends, those times she'd wakened dazed and sickish and not knowing where she was, possibly such things had been done to her. She'd forgotten. These were bad habits for a girl Katya's age, but no habit is so bad it can't be forgotten, erased. There were guys — older guys — she'd yearned for so frankly you could see it

[27]

in her face. She'd hoped they would love her, but that was silly. Not enough for Katya Spivak that these guys wanted her sexually; any guy might want her sexually. Badly she wanted them to love her: Katya Spivak. To tell her that she was special to them, not just any girl. Badly she wanted her cousin Roy Mraz to love her and to respect her.

Roy Mraz was Katya's "distant" cousin, and possibly they were not blood relations, for the woman known as Roy's mother was in fact Roy's stepmother, and it was this stepmother to whom Katya's mother, Essie, was related. *Stay away from those people,* Katya's mother warned. Roy was twenty-two. Lately he'd returned to Vineland from eighteen months in Glassboro. In Glassboro he'd acquired "tats": tattoos. He'd acquired bad habits, of which Katya did not want to think. And he did not care for her; Katya was too young for him and not sexy or good-looking enough. *The hell with him. Why should I feel bad about him!* She was in Bayhead Harbor for July and August, and she could have wept, she was so grateful. Almost she'd cried when the rich lady from Saddle River called, saying, *Katya? If you're still free . . .*

The Engelhardts demanded a good deal from their live-in nanny and from their live-in housekeeper, this was true, but they were paying Katya more than she'd ever been paid in Vineland. And she was in Bayhead Harbor, on the Jersey shore, and not in Vineland, which was steamy hot in the summer. And there was the split-level on the channel, and Mr. Engelhardt's thirty-foot Chris-Craft powerboat she'd described to her mother and sisters on the phone, and there were the Engelhardt children — Tricia, baby Kevin. Her mother had warned, *Don't get attached to kids — that's a mistake.* Meaning the kids of people you worked for. Katya was not likely to make that mistake. Still, the baby's moist, sudden smile, that shine in his eyes when he saw her — those took Katya's breath away. Better when they were being bratty. Spoiled, demanding. Better when Mrs. Engelhardt spoke sharply to her with that knife-blade frown between her penciled

eyebrows: *Katya! Come here, please. Katya! Do this again, please.*
Yet here was the nanny's secret: she'd been invited to the home
of Marcus Kidder, who was one of the really rich residents of
Bayhead Harbor, with a mansion-sized house on the Atlantic
Ocean, and the Engelhardts had not. Sneeringly Marcus Kidder had spoken of "mayflies." You could see, it was bred into
Mr. Kidder to look down upon others who were his social inferi-
ors, and this looking-down-upon-others was pleasing to Katya, as
revenge.

To a man like Marcus Kidder, the difference between the
Engelhardts and the Spivaks wasn't that great, Katya thought. *We
are all inferior to him, you can see.* Katya liked this. If a wealthy
man is your friend, you can see his point of view.

What was disturbing about Marcus Kidder, Katya thought, was
that he could see into her heart. Did she dare to lie to Mr. Kidder? Would he laugh at her if she tried? (As children are laughed
at when they clumsily lie, for lying is a skill you have to learn!)
Katya liked to think that she'd become a skilled and accomplished and at times seductive liar, but she couldn't convince
herself that Marcus Kidder would believe her if she tried to lie to
him, and so: did Katya dare to return to him? To that house?

Dear Katya! You know, you don't need to tell anyone. Somehow
he'd known that it was the red lace lingerie Katya had been looking at in the store window, and not the demure white nightgown.
Don't need to tell anyone was what men said, wanting to share a
sex secret with a teenager.

There'd been adult men in Katya Spivak's life. Older men
whose ages Katya could only guess at. One of the mechanics
in her uncle Fritzie's garage had smiled at Katya, drawing his
tongue slowly across his fat lower lip, had said certain words to
her that were near-inaudible and frightening; and Katya had
never told anyone, of course. And there was Artie, one of Katya's
mother's friends, who'd offered Katya a ride home from school
one day when Katya was twelve years old, and something in his

face, something in his jovial, drunk-sounding voice — *Hey, Katya, c'mon, climb in, don't be shy, sweetheart* — warned her: *No.*

Never tell Momma her man friend had been looking at Katya *in that way.*

And now, had Marcus Kidder looked at Katya *in that way?* Difficult to know, for Marcus Kidder was wholly unlike any of the Vineland men, of any age. But the red lace lingerie! Katya was not a girl to wear such lingerie and be stared at like one of those exotic dancers on billboards above the Garden State Parkway advertising Atlantic City casinos, and Katya was not a girl to be laughed at as guys like Roy Mraz would laugh at her. Roy Mraz had sucked Katya's lower lip into his mouth (in play? rough play?) and Katya had panicked, for what if Roy had chewed off her lip like a rat, what if crazy Roy, high on crystal meth, had swallowed Katya's lip? He'd enticed Katya into sniffing up into her nostrils and so up into her brain the bitter white chemical-smelling powder, and what she'd inhaled had been fiery and awful and her vision had become blotched and watery and (possibly) she'd blacked out and fallen a long, long distance and so (possibly) certain things were done to her by Roy Mraz which Katya could not think of clearly, still less comprehend, as if she were trying to recall scenes of a TV movie of long ago seen late at night in exhaustion and confused circumstances. Snorting — "snorting ice" — it was something you did, or, somehow, something that was done to you as in appalled fascination you watched yourself at a distance of about ten feet, a limp raggedy-doll figure with a slack, smeared mouth and glazed eyes. This was Katya's secret! Katya's secret, and yet somehow (how?) there came her mother, rushing at her to slap Katya's face and scream, *What did I tell you! What the hell did I tell you! Stay away from the Mrazes! All that side of the family!* So Essic Spivak spoke in fear and loathing of her own relatives, for she knew them, Essie said, as few others did, from the inside out.

In Bayhead Harbor, none of that mattered. Spivak, Mraz — these south Jersey/Pine Barrens names meant nothing. Waking early before dawn in this new bed, Katya's first thought was, *No one knows me here,* which should have been a consolation but in fact left her feeling adrift, bereft. Homesick?

It was seagulls that woke her so early. Piercing cries confused her dreams. Cries of hunger that sounded like cries of pain, rage. As in Vineland often she was wakened by crows at the landfill nearby, where raw garbage was dumped. A crow is weirdly human, Katya thought. You can hear crows laughing with one another, rowdy and jeering like drunken men. At the dead end of County Line Road, where the Cumberland County landfill sprawled across several acres, you could see swarms of crows, red-tailed hawks, turkey vultures, descending from the sky, flapping their fake-looking wings like oversized bats. Katya's brothers, Dewayne and Ralph, shot their .22-caliber rifles at these garbage birds, as they called them, popping them out of the sky. In the landfill Katya had tramped eagerly after her long-legged brothers, searching for treasure when she'd been a little girl.

Katya, here! Somethin' for you.

A big baby doll with wide-open glass eyes, a rosebud mouth.

Propped atop a mound of refuse. Before Katya could run to it, the baby doll's rubber head burst and disappeared into nothingness when the rifles discharged.

Hey, Katya, don't cry. That wasn't no clean baby doll, that was a damn dirty ol' doll some nigger girl cast out.

Now Katya was in Bayhead Harbor, and here treasure was everywhere. In the glittering store windows of Ocean Avenue, in the gleaming luxury vehicles cruising the shaded streets, glimpsed through openings in privet hedges. You could see it at a distance, you could admire and envy it, and yet you dared not touch it; such treasure is forbidden to you.

4

HERE WAS A SURPRISE: Mr. Kidder was not only an artist but a writer. Of children's books, at least.

Only after they'd returned from their tea-time at Mr. Kidder's house and Katya had found time to sit down with Tricia and read *Funny Bunny's Birthday Party* to her did she discover that Mr. Kidder had given Tricia his own book: that is, Marcus Cullen Kidder was both the author and the illustrator.

Katya was embarrassed. She hadn't so much as glanced at the name on the colorful book cover when she'd taken it from Tricia. It was like Mr. Kidder — modesty and vanity so mixed, you could not distinguish one from the other — not to have hinted that the book was his. Katya turned to the title page, where in a flowing script in purple ink Mr. Kidder had inscribed the book *To Tricia, in the fervent hope that she will never change.* Mr. Kidder's signature was such a flourish of the pen you'd have had to know that the scrawled name was Marcus Cullen Kidder to decipher it.

Tricia adored *Funny Bunny.* Tricia could not get enough of *Funny Bunny.* Tricia insisted that Katya read it to her again and yet again. The best part of being a nanny, Katya thought, was reading children's books aloud to enraptured children like Tricia, for no one had read such books aloud to her when she'd been a little girl. There hadn't been such books in the Spivak household on County Line Road, nor would there have been any time for such interludes. Katya had to concede that Funny Bunny was a wonderfully cuddly plump white rabbit with upright pink ears, a pink nose, appealing shiny brown eyes. As the artist depicted him, Funny Bunny was funny without knowing it; you could laugh at Funny Bunny, though not meanly. Funny Bunny had many worries and all of them were imaginary. His greatest worry was that everyone had forgotten his birthday, but in fact all of his brothers and sisters and animal friends in the woods had prepared a surprise birthday party for him which left Funny Bunny with many wonderful gifts (among them — Katya smiled; Marcus Kidder was so clever — a magician's top hat, for Funny Bunny to disappear into when he wished to hide) but, more important, made him realize that he had many friends who cared for him. The final drawing showed Funny Bunny at bedtime in a drowsy tangle of brother and sister bunnies: "And so Funny Bunny knew he was never alone for a minute, even when he thought he was."

Katya thought, *Whoever wrote such a story has a beautiful soul.*

"Katya, what is this? This — *Funny Bunny's Birthday Party?*" Mrs. Engelhardt had discovered the book and was leafing through it, frowning. "Where did Tricia get this book?"

Carefully Katya explained that the author himself had given it to Tricia; that was his signature inside. He lived in Bayhead Harbor.

And Mrs. Engelhardt turned to the title page and read the inscription and puzzled over the wild scrawl of the signature. "Kidder! Kidder is a prominent name in Bayhead Harbor, I think. Isn't there a Kidder Memorial somewhere — the library? Isn't it named for that family? Where did you meet Mr. Kidder — at the library?" It was like Mrs. Engelhardt to speak rapidly, to ask and to answer her own questions, but Katya said, "In Harbor Park. We were feeding geese . . . Mr. Kidder is a white-haired old man, and very sweet."

Distractedly Mrs. Engelhardt leafed through the picture book, examining the highly detailed, striking drawings of Funny Bunny and his companions. If Mrs. Engelhardt had not been expecting houseguests within the hour and been involved in preparing a dinner party for ten that evening at the house, she might have had more than a vague interest in Bayhead Harbor resident Marcus Kidder and exactly how he'd come to give her daughter the book. "Signed with the author's signature — this might be a collector's item one day . . ." Ordinarily Mrs. Engelhardt was given to suspect that her good nature and her trust were being subtly betrayed by persons in her employ, unless she was vigilant; she had to keep a sharp eye on both her live-in housekeeper and her live-in nanny. But she was pleased with Katya now, and smiled at her with such genuine feeling, Katya felt a thrill of affection for her employer, who was not so bad after all and with whom she might — almost, in another context — be friends. Here was a triumph for Lorraine Engelhardt: a beautiful children's book signed by the author, inscribed to her daughter. In weeks to come, frequently Katya would observe Lorraine showing *Funny Bunny's Birthday Party* to visitors, proudly opening it to the title page.

Now she said to Katya, "Tricia should write this dear old man a thank-you note. I mean, we should write. Could you take care of this, Katya? Buy a nice card at the drugstore and write a nice note and help Tricia to 'sign' her name. Be sure to include our address and telephone number, in case Mr. Kidder wants to respond. I'm sure that you can find his address in the telephone directory, or from a librarian at the library."

Katya said happily, "Yes, Mrs. Engelhardt. I will."

5

THIS TIME KATYA didn't pause to ring Mr. Kidder's doorbell.

It was Wednesday afternoon, Katya's half-day off. On her way to the beach she was stopping by 17 Proxmire Street to take the thank-you note from Tricia Engelhardt in person. Out of colorful construction paper she and the little girl had made a thank-you card, and in crayon, with Katya guiding her shaky little hand, Tricia had signed her name. Katya was pleased with their work, though on her way out of the house, Mrs. Engelhardt had had time merely to glance at it. Katya smiled, thinking, *I will deliver it by hand.*

Vowed she would not return to that house, but now it was happening. *Would not* transformed to *would* as naturally as the happy resolution of Funny Bunny's worries.

As she pushed through the wrought-iron gate, she began to hear a piano being played somewhere inside the shingleboard house. This time the pianist paused repeatedly in his playing, broke off and began again impatiently. Impulsively Katya left the flagstone path, circled the house on the damp grassy lawn, and found herself at the rear, right-hand corner of the house, where, through a screened window, she saw white-haired Mr. Kidder seated at a piano, his back to her. Picking at the keyboard, playing briefly with both hands and then abruptly stopping . . . Katya liked it: clever Marcus Kidder had no idea that anyone was spying on *him.*

Another roll of the dice — this felt right.

Go with your gut, gamblers know. And this Katya Spivak knew.

She was wearing her swimsuit beneath a pair of white shorts and a blue Bayhead Harbor Yacht Club T-shirt passed on to her by Mrs. Engelhardt because it was too small for Katya's employer's fleshy shoulders and breasts. She'd brushed her streaked-blond hair until it shone, and she was wearing flashy jade studs in her ears. She liked it that Marcus Kidder would be surprised to see her, and that it seemed to be a casual thing for Katya to drop by 17 Proxmire Street, as if the impressive house behind the privet hedge were a natural stop for a nanny from south Jersey on her way to the public beach.

Katya stood in the grass listening to Mr. Kidder at the piano. She was carrying a bulky straw bag, the thank-you note inside. She loved the sensation of being unseen, the thrill of trespassing on a rich man's property without his knowing. Through the window screen she saw how, when Mr. Kidder ceased playing the piano, he leaned forward to scribble something on a stiff sheet of paper. She thought, *He is a composer, too. He composes music,* and the realization seemed wonderful to her, magical.

Softly Katya called to him: "Hel-lo, Mr. Kid-der."

Comical to see how surprised the white-haired old man was! Katya laughed as he turned to her, astonished. He was wearing glasses with chunky black frames, which he hurriedly removed. "Why, Katya! Is that you?"

He stumbled to open a door. Katya stood hesitantly in the grass, saying she didn't want to disturb him, she'd brought something to deliver to him.

"Something — for me?" Mr. Kidder stood in the doorway, frowning and smiling, gazing at Katya with that melting sick-sinking look that left Katya feeling faint, lightheaded herself. *He wants me, this old man.* Desire and yearning in Mr. Kidder's startled blue eyes were like nothing Katya saw in the eyes of other, younger men, like Roy Mraz.

But Mr. Kidder managed to compose himself. You could see

the transformation as if a spotlight had been turned upon an actor. "You've forgiven me, Katya dear? I was hoping you would."

Katya laughed, feeling a hot, pleasurable blush rise in her face. "No! I have not. I'm only here for a few minutes on my way to . . ." In the confusion of the moment, Katya had forgotten where she was going.

"Come in! If but 'for a few minutes,' each minute will be precious."

To enter the house, Katya had to brush close by Mr. Kidder, who stood just inside the doorway, holding the screen door open. She was uncomfortably aware of his closeness: his height, the warmth that lifted from his skin, his quickened breathing, a faint scent of cologne. At least, Katya thought the scent must be cologne. As if possibly Mr. Kidder had been expecting a visitor this afternoon, he wasn't wearing beltless khaki shorts but pale beige linen trousers and a pale green shirt of some fine-woven fabric; on his feet, the sporty white yachtsman's shoes. He was clean-shaven; the floating white hair was not disheveled. Katya thought that he might grasp her hands in his, he might try to kiss her, but she slipped past him.

Exhilarated, she thought, *He wants me! Me, me!*

Katya found herself in a room of surpassing beauty — a "drawing room"? At its center was a gleaming cream-colored grand piano, the largest Katya had ever seen.

"It's a concert grand, Katya. But I assure you, my playing is far from grand."

Katya laughed. She could think of no reply to Mr. Kidder's remark. In her fevered imagination of the past twenty-four hours, she'd rehearsed what she might say to Marcus Kidder, but in these scenarios only Katya spoke, not Mr. Kidder.

Out of her straw bag Katya took the handmade card. "This is for you, Mr. Kidder. From Tricia Engelhardt, who adores *Funny Bunny* and has made me read it to her a dozen times already."

[37]

The envelope of red construction paper was decorated with animal stickers. Mr. Kidder took it from Katya with a perplexed smile. You could see he had no idea who Tricia Engelhardt was. But when he removed the card and read the thank-you note Katya had composed, he was stricken with sudden emotion. "Why, this is a . . . work of art. This is" — to Katya's dismay, he spoke haltingly, brushing at his eyes with his fingertips — "very beautiful."

Katya stared. It was weakness in adults she hated, that frightened her.

Her grandfather Spivak had been a prison guard at Glassboro for nearly thirty years. He'd ruined his health with smoking, heavy drinking; he shuffled when he walked, as if broken-backed; but he wasn't weak. Never would he have been stricken with emotion like this, for something so trivial. And Katya's father, whom she had not seen in some time, would never have displayed such weakness before witnesses. She was sure!

Boldly, Katya prowled about the room. She scarcely listened to the white-haired man's halting speech; she'd have liked to press her hands over her ears. Here was a room of surpassing beauty, she thought. Not cluttered and smelling of paint and turpentine like Mr. Kidder's studio but furnished with beautiful things like a show window. The floor was polished hardwood — parket? — par*kay*? — and over it lay a large oval Oriental rug of a dark dusty-rose color. Surrounding the piano were sofas with brightly colored pillows, white wicker chairs, lamps with flaring white shades. On the walls, grass green wallpaper: silk? On the mantel above a wide white brick fireplace were vases containing glass flowers — Mr. Kidder's fossil flowers — of striking colors and shapes. There was a stereo set in a carved mahogany cabinet, and there were shelves of records so tightly crammed together that Katya's head ached to see them. So much music! And none of Mr. Kidder's music, she seemed to know, would be familiar to her.

Solemnly she said, "This is a very beautiful room, Mr. Kidder. I think this must be a special room."

"Yes it is, dear. At the moment."

Dear! She smiled.

At the Engelhardts' house, Katya Spivak was invisible. Unless Mrs. Engelhardt suddenly spoke to her, with a quick hard smile and a request, or a reprimand. In her own household in Vineland, Katya Spivak was likely to be even less visible, for often there was no one home: her mother's work hours shifted mysteriously. But here in Mr. Kidder's drawing room, Katya Spivak was wholly visible.

Conscious of Mr. Kidder watching her as she moved about the room like a curious child. Conscious at the same time of her ponytail swinging between her shoulder blades, her smooth tanned legs springy and taut as a dancer's legs. In the mirror above the mantel there was a very pretty young girl with streaked-blond hair and a daring red slash of a mouth, thrilling to see. And in the corner of her eye Katya saw, or believed she saw, Mr. Kidder moving toward her. She steeled herself for the man's touch, his embrace; she would push away from him if he tried to embrace her. But she felt instead only a tentative stroke of her ponytail. She did not turn around but moved away as if not noticing. And when she went to peer curiously at a shelf of records (all Mozart? Katya was sure she'd never heard any of Mozart's music), she saw, to her surprise, that Mr. Kidder hadn't moved and could not have touched her hair; he was only gazing at her with a smile of longing. In his hand was the construction-paper card, which he seemed to be taking so seriously. He said, "Of course I remember dear Tricia. And you are Tricia's nanny, and you are obviously the creator of this card for Marcus Cullen Kidder, which he will prize forever."

Now Katya understood that Mr. Kidder was joking: the wistful old-man yearning, the maudlin words, were meant to be funny.

Katya laughed, to indicate she got the joke. "Oh, *sure.*"

She drew her fingertips along the piano keyboard, provoking a blurred discordant sound. Above the keyboard was the name

Rameau in gilt letters. "Wish I could play piano. I'd have liked that," she said, in a glib, flat voice that suggested insincerity, though in fact she was sincere, or meant to be at that moment. And Mr. Kidder said, almost too eagerly, "But it isn't too late, Katya, surely . . ." Among Katya's many relatives scattered through south Jersey she could think of no one at all musical except one or two boy cousins who played, or tried to play, amplified guitar.

Katya examined music books stacked on Mr. Kidder's piano, most of them looking well-worn: *Collected Piano Pieces of Ravel, Chopin: Ballads, Schubert: Lieder, Collected Piano Music of George Gershwin, Spellbound Concerto* by Miklós Rózsa, *In the Still of the Night: Love Songs of Cole Porter, Harold Arlen: A Treasure* . . . Against the music stand were sheets of paper which Mr. Kidder had been annotating, in pencil. "Mr. Kidder, are you writing music? — your own music?" Katya asked, intrigued. "Composing music?" In her nasal Jersey accent the question sounded faintly jeering.

Stiffly Mr. Kidder said no. He was not.

He took the annotated sheets from the piano, stacked them together, and laid them on a shelf. He seemed offended, embarrassed. Katya could not see how she'd insulted him. With girlish naiveté, she said, "Play something for me, Mr. Kidder? Like what you were playing just now?"

"I told you *no,* Katya."

No, Katya. She felt rebuked as a child.

A flush had come into Mr. Kidder's face, a flush of annoyance. His eyes were not so tender now. So quickly an adult can turn — an adult man especially. Katya knew; Katya had had certain experiences. You can be on easy terms with such a man, you can see that he likes you, then by mistake you say the wrong word or make the wrong assumption and something shuts down in his face. Like an iron grating over a pawnshop window on a rundown street in Atlantic City. That abrupt.

Mr. Kidder relented. "In fact, I've been trying to compose lie-

der, Katya. But my efforts aren't yet worthy of being heard by anyone, including you."

Katya smiled, perplexed. *Lieder?*

"It's German — songs. Usually love songs."

Love songs! Katya smiled foolishly and could not think of a
reply. Mr. Kidder was asking what sort of music she liked, and
Katya tried to think: Radiohead? Guns N' Roses? Nine Inch
Nails? Pearl Jam? Nirvana? Evasively she said, "Nothing special,
Mr. Kidder. Nothing you'd like, I guess."

Katya turned her attention to the many framed photographs
on the grass green walls, which she'd assumed might depict
members of Mr. Kidder's family: except these were glossy glamour photos of women who looked as if they were in show business, heavily made up, hair styled in the exaggerated fashions of
long-ago times. Katya saw that each of the photos was inscribed
To Marcus Kidder with love: from Carol Channing, Sandy Duncan, Bernadette Peters, Angela Lansbury, Lauren Bacall, Tammy
Grimes. Katya asked if these glamorous women were friends of
Mr. Kidder's and Mr. Kidder said, "No, dear. No longer."

A pertly pretty red-haired woman smiled at the viewer over
her bare shoulder above the gaily scrawled inscription *For dearest Marcus with much much love & kisses, Gwen April 1957.*

"That's Gwen Verdon," Mr. Kidder said. "She was the toast of
Broadway in the 1950s and beyond, but you have not heard of
her, Katya, I'm sure."

Katya mumbled an inaudible reply. So remote in time, April
1957; it made her feel lightheaded.

Mr. Kidder said, "For a while I was a Broadway investor. I'd
studied at Juilliard, I'd had naive hopes for a musical career myself. Music has always been one of my loves, like art — mostly un-
requited loves. Though overall I didn't do badly as an investor. I
may have broken even." He spoke with that air of ironic wistful-
ness that Katya disliked.

She asked if he'd been in love with any of these women and

Mr. Kidder said *no*, certainly not. And Katya asked why not, and Mr. Kidder said, "Because I'm not attracted to glamour, dear Katya. I am a dilettante and a collector and a lover — of beauty. But glamour and beauty are very different things."

Katya wanted to ask him about his wife — wives. His children, if he had any. So mysterious he seemed to her, though baring his soul in a way no self-respecting man would do, in Katya's experience.

She thought, *He wants to do something to me. In his head, he is doing things to me.* Yet the curious thrill of trespass held her captive, and she could not break away.

Now Mr. Kidder did touch Katya's ponytail, gently. His fingers were light on the nape of her neck, and she shivered involuntarily, laughed, and eased away, gripping the bulky straw bag to hold between them.

"You are thinking that I have some sort of design on you, dear Katya! I know, I can read your thoughts, which show so clearly, so purely, in your face. And you are correct, dear: I do have a design on you. I have a mission for you, I think! If you are indeed the one."

"What do you mean? 'The one'?" Katya stammered, not knowing whether this was serious or one of Mr. Kidder's enigmatic jokes.

"A fair maiden — to be entrusted with a crucial task. For which she would be handsomely rewarded, in time."

Katya stood gripping the straw bag to her chest. Frightened, and confused. And yet her heart beat quickly in anticipation.

"There's a German term — *heimweh*, homesickness. It's a powerful sensation, like a narcotic. A yearning for home, but for something more — a past self, perhaps. A lost self. When I first saw you on the street, Katya, I felt such a sensation . . . I have no idea why."

Now Mr. Kidder spoke urgently, sincerely. Holding both his hands out to Katya, palms up in a gesture of appeal. Still Katya stood unmoving, gripping her bag. She could think of no way of replying to Mr. Kidder that would not have struck a clumsy note: her instinctive reaction was to laugh nervously, stammer something stupidly adolescent, back away . . . It was an extraordinary sensation, to be *looked at* by a stranger, as if he were peering into her very soul.

"Well. I don't mean to frighten you, dear. I am perfectly harmless, I promise! This mission is not now . . . will not be revealed for a while — we need not think of it now. We have other things to think of now." Mr. Kidder smiled, and lightly touched Katya's wrist as if to break the spell. "Before you leave, dear, let me play something for you. Some music I hope you will like. A young relative of mine, a tenor . . ."

Mr. Kidder removed a record from one of the shelves, placed it on a turntable. Such antiquated things! Katya sat in one of the white wicker chairs, at the edge of the brightly colored cushion, uneasy. She thought, *This is a test. He is testing me,* thinking how badly she wanted to flee this house, how distrustful she was of Marcus Kidder really.

A young man's voice sounded suddenly, high, pure, beautiful. As intimate in Katya's ears as if the singer were in the room with them.

> *In Scarlet Town, where I was born*
> *There was a fair maid dwelling.*
> *Made every youth cry well-a-day!*
> *Her name was Barbara Allen.*
>
> *All in the merry month of May*
> *When green buds they were swelling,*
> *Young Jeremy Grove on his deathbed lay*
> *For love of Barbara Allen.*
>
> *He sent his man unto her then . . .*

Closely Katya listened, scarcely daring to breathe. The singer had such a pure voice, beautifully modulated yet masculine. The words of the song seemed to pierce her heart. An old song, a song of long ago — a song Katya's friends in Vineland would have sneered at, as, in their company, Katya herself would have sneered at it.

> *So slowly, slowly, she came up*
> *And slowly she came nigh him.*
> *And all she said when there she came,*
> *"Young man, I think you're dying."*

> *As she was walking o'er the fields*
> *She heard the death bell knelling.*
> *And every stroke did seem to say,*
> *Hardhearted Barbara Allen.*

Hardhearted Barbara Allen! Katya felt a thrill of cruel satisfaction. She liked it that Barbara Allen had told the sick/weak young man to die; and what exhilaration, to realize such power.

Yet the song continued; the young male singer had not yet finished his tale. Katya sat now tensely at the edge of her seat, gripping her hands together on her bare knees. Shadows through a latticed window moved restlessly against a wall, appearing, disappearing. Distractedly, Katya thought there must be birds in the shrubbery just outside.

> *"Oh Mother, Mother, make my bed*
> *Make it long and narrow.*
> *Sweet Jeremy died for love of me,*
> *And I will die of sorrow."*

> *They buried her in the old churchyard*
> *Sweet Jeremy's grave nigh hers.*

And from his grave grew a red, red rose
And from hers grew a cruel briar.

This was a surprise. Katya listened anxiously, not wanting the song to end. Yet the young singer concluded, in a voice of melancholy authority:

They grew and grew up the old church spire
Till they couldn't grow any higher.
And there they twined in a true love knot,
The red rose and the green briar.

There was a final refrain, purely music. Until now Katya had scarcely been aware of the musical accompaniment, a delicate-sounding stringed instrument. And the record was old, marred with scratching.

Her eyes stung with tears. This was ridiculous. It was only an old song, and yet Katya was close to crying.

Mr. Kidder rose and removed the record from the turntable. He regarded Katya with mild surprise, as if he hadn't expected her to listen so closely to the song, or to be so emotionally engaged.

Katya wiped at her eyes and asked brightly, "Who is the singer? Someone in your family, you said?"

"Yes. Did you like his voice?"

Katya nodded. Emphatically: yes.

"Would you like to meet him, dear? Someday?"

More guardedly, Katya nodded. For this might be one of Marcus Kidder's little jokes, she knew.

Gravely he said, "And the singer would like — would have liked — to meet you. In the recording, he is twenty years old."

Katya could not bring herself to ask when the recording had been made. Clearly it was old, of another era, before CDs and iPods. Mr. Kidder said, "In 1945."

Katya tried to smile. "Who —?" and Mr. Kidder said with a little grimace, *"Moi."* Again Katya asked, "Who?" and Mr. Kidder said, "Marcus Kidder, promising young tenor, 1945. You have heard both his recording debut and the pinnacle of his career." Mr. Kidder bowed his head playfully, hand to his shirtfront. The pale green shirt was unbuttoned at the throat; in the V a swath of thin silvery gray hair bristled.

Quickly Katya said, "The song is very beautiful, Mr. Kidder. You had — you have — a beautiful voice." She was trying to keep shock and disappointment off her face.

Mr. Kidder laughed. He returned the record to the shelf, shoving it into a crammed space. *"Had,* dear. Not *have.* That hopeful young tenor is long vanished. If I tried to sing 'Barbara Allen' now, I would sound like an aged crow."

Katya was on her feet, desperate to leave. She thanked Mr. Kidder for playing the record, stammered that she had to go, someone was waiting for her at the beach . . . Such pity she felt for Marcus Kidder, a physical revulsion for him, she could hardly bear to meet his eyes. She allowed him to squeeze her hand in farewell, then pulled from him.

At the door he called after her, "Katya, wait. Your little gift from Prim Rose Lane — I promised it would be waiting for you, and so it is. If —"

But Katya was walking quickly away. Called back over her shoulder that she didn't want it. Half ran to the little gateway in the privet hedge and along Proxmire Street. The public beach was a ten-minute walk, and by the time Katya got to it, she was breathless and indignant. *Asshole! Playing one of your damn tricks on me.* She pulled off her T-shirt, her shorts. In a red-striped bottom and halter top, she strode along the beach, into the surf. Just to get her legs wet felt good. The breezy ocean air felt good. And there on his lifeguard perch was darkly tanned Doug, a local guy she'd hoped would be on duty again this week who would call out to her with a shark-flash of a smile, "Katie! Hi."

6

FROWNING, MRS. ENGELHARDT said, "A call for you, Katya."

In apprehension Katya took the phone, for the caller could only be her mother. Katya had given the Engelhardts' number to no one else, and she'd asked her mother not to call her except in an emergency, so she steeled herself now for bad news. In an alcove off the Engelhardts' kitchen, she heard her mother's aggrieved and reproachful voice on the line without grasping at first what she was saying; she was demanding to know why Katya hadn't called for so long. And Katya protested that she had called only a few days ago, and Katya's mother said suspiciously, "Can't you talk? Is someone listening?" and Katya said, "No! I can't talk now because I'm working, Momma," and Katya's mother interrupted, saying, "Is something going on up there? What is going on up there?" speaking rapidly and not very coherently, and Katya stammered, "What do you mean, Momma? You know I'm working, I'm working as a nanny, I have two small children to look after —" and Katya's mother said sharply, "Don't talk to me that way, Katya! I'm calling to ask how those people are treating you. Eggenstein — that's a Jewish name, right? Are they paying you what they promised? Are they paying you on time?" and Katya, pressing the receiver tight against her ear in fear that her mother's voice might be overheard by Mrs. Engelhardt, only a few yards away in the kitchen with the Hispanic housekeeper, weakly protested, "Momma, look, I can't — can't talk right now. We're going to the b-beach —" and Katya's mother laughed harshly. "Going to the beach — la-di-*da!* Last time it was going out on the yacht. Some of us have to work at this hour of the morning," and

[47]

in some desperation Katya asked if there was any special reason for her to be calling, and Katya's mother said furiously, "Special reason — goddamn, *yes*. I am your goddamned mother, and I am concerned about you, for Christ's sake. How do I know what the hell you're doing there in Bayhead! You're too damned trusting, too good-looking for your own damned good, and underage, which means you can get picked up for drinking. Don't try to tell me you don't smoke dope, I know you do, don't lie to *me*. Remember Yvette, what happened to her —" And so Katya had to steel herself for a grim recitation of what had happened to her mother's younger sister at the age of eighteen, waitressing at a resort hotel in Cape May, saving to go to nursing school, but she got involved with a young man who was a student at Rutgers in New Brunswick, "got pregnant and got dumped," as Katya's mother never failed to recall in harsh staccato disapproval mingled with satisfaction — "people like that, they treat you like shit" — and Katya said, "Right, Momma — yes, I know. You've told me plenty of times, I know. But right now —" and Katya's mother said, "Can you swear they're not cheating you? These Eggensteins," and Katya said, lowering her voice, "Engelhardt, Momma. I wrote the name down for you — you have all the information," and Katya's mother said, "You! You don't have good judgment. Look how trusting you were with Roy — damned lucky you didn't get in serious trouble with that bastard," and Katya swallowed hard and did not speak, would not speak. "D'you know Roy is back in Vineland? Working at the garage. I ran into him the other night and first thing he says is, 'Where's Katya?'" and Katya's heart kicked, a sick-sinking sensation in her gut, but she was determined not to inquire about Roy Mraz, never would she inquire about Roy Mraz, fuck Roy Mraz; and Katya's mother was asking about the Eggenstein children, how was Katya getting along with them, and Katya said that she was getting along very well with them, with all of the Engelhardts, this was the best summer job she'd ever had, the little girl was so sweet, only just a little spoiled but sweet, and the little boy was just a baby; and this provoked Katya's mother to flare up indignantly, saying, "Didn't I tell you, Katya — don't get attached to people like that, that is a terrible mistake to get attached to somebody else's children when your own goddamned children are enough to break your heart."

And now, belatedly, Katya was made to realize that her mother was drunk, and in no mood to be contradicted or even reasoned with; and Katya was anxious, seeing that Mrs. Engelhardt was peering out at her through the kitchen doorway. Mrs. Engelhardt was naturally suspicious of any employee receiving telephone calls during the day, during her "hours," for she was being paid to work for the Engelhardts during these "hours," though at least the caller was the girl's mother and not a boy or a man — that, Mrs. Engelhardt would not allow. (And disapproving this morning of Katya, who'd returned to the house after eleven o'clock the night before, letting herself into her room on the ground floor with her key, quietly, it might've been stealthily, as Mrs. Engelhardt lay upstairs in her bed listening closely to determine if the nanny from south Jersey was bringing anyone back to the house with her, a boy, a man — any stranger was forbidden on the premises — but Katya was alone, Katya was defiantly thinking, *It's my half-day off, I have a right*, though knowing that Mrs. Engelhardt disapproved of her staying out past 9 P.M., imagined her drinking, smoking dope, partying with boys. How much more Mrs. Engelhardt would have preferred a hired girl who didn't attract boys or men and who stayed close to the house even on her days off, watching late-night TV movies with Mrs. Engelhardt weeknights when Mr. Engelhardt was in the city working.)

"— listening, Katya? You're so quiet! Why I called, it *is* an emergency. Can you send me a money order for three hundred dollars? I need it by —" and Katya was too stunned to follow this, asked her mother to repeat what she'd said.

"You must have some money saved by now, Katya, it's been two weeks, two weeks' pay, you could ask those people there,

Eggensteins, for the rest of it, explain it's a family emergency, honey, which it is."

Katya stood listening in dismay to her mother's pleading and yet reproachful words, through a roar of blood pulsing in her ears, for as her mother continued to speak, it developed that she wasn't in Vineland but in Atlantic City and Katya would have to mail the money order to her there. She was in the Silverado Motel on Eleventh Street, where she'd gone with "my friend Ethel" — unless it was "my friend Edsel" — and there was some misunderstanding about the motel bill, and "wear and tear" to the room, and the manager she'd thought was her friend was now threatening to call the police, and if so, Essie Spivak would be arrested and get prison time, and Katya couldn't let that happen to her mother, could she? "Honey, I'm desperate. It was a mistake to come here, but I got talked into it and now, this motel bill, it's a mistake but what can I do, it's like blackmail, honey, I'm fucked if they call the cops, you know that —"

When Katya was twelve years old her mother had been arrested for forging checks. Essie and certain of her friends had fallen into the habit of borrowing from Pay Day Loans, which charged such high interest rates, crazily high interest, like 11 percent? 12 percent? This was when Essie worked weekends at the Mirage Casino in Atlantic City as a blackjack girl; she developed a drinking habit, a codeine habit, borrowed money from men friends and from Pay Day Loans and then more money to repay the high interest and at last, in desperation, she forged checks. She was immediately caught at a 7-Eleven in Vineland and arrested, taken away to jail, booked, and she pleaded guilty and was sentenced by a county judge to eighteen months' probation. But now, if Essie Spivak was arrested again, her old record would be held against her, she'd be sent to Glassboro State Facility for Women.

"I will kill myself first, Katya! I promise I will! You won't let that happen, honey, will you? As soon as I'm paid what is owed me — there are people here who owe *me* — I'll send a check to you right there in Bayhead, honey. I swear I will. Put that Mrs. Eggstein on the phone, let me explain to her, she's a mother like me, it's a family emergency, a medical emergency, which is no goddamned lie, three hundred dollars will be repaid with interest. Honey, help me! I need your help. I love you, Katya" — sobbing now, pleading and desperate and yet still aggrieved, angry — " — my only girl left now, my only baby, the others have grown up and moved away and don't give a shit about their mother, that they have broken her heart —" and Katya said, "All right, Momma. Give me the address there."

Heimweh: was that the word? Homesickness.

In Bayhead Harbor she'd missed home. Yet she was never so homesick as when she was home in the house on County Line Road in Vineland.

She'd have liked to ask Mr. Kidder about this. How you could be homesick when you were home . . .

For it was an earlier time, before Katya's father had left, that she missed. She'd been only nine when he'd disappeared from their lives, and only vaguely could she remember Daddy lifting her in his arms, laughing at her frightened expression, calling her "Pretty Baby" and kissing her, promising her he'd be back for her birthday, but the worst of it was, Daddy had been so often away, returning and then leaving again, and it was a secret where Daddy was when he was gone — unless Katya's mother blurted out in drunken fury that Daddy was staying with another woman — and then gradually it became a fact that Daddy was gone. And Katya asked, *Gone where?* and the answer was blunt and ungiving: *Gone.*

SPRINGDALE PUBLIC LIBRARY
405 S. Pleasant
Springdale, AR 72764

7

SHE KNEW: this was a mistake.

Even before the knife-blade frown appeared between Mrs. Engelhardt's dark-penciled eyebrows.

Katya spoke of a "family emergency," a "medical emergency," and at once her employer became upset, indignant: "Katya, you aren't leaving us, are you? We are counting on you" — for Mrs. Engelhardt was a woman to seize an emotion and wrest it from you and run with it, appropriating it as her own, to intimidate and confound — "at this time in mid-July we couldn't possibly replace you with another girl." So that Katya was forced to say quickly, apologetically, "No, no — I'm not leaving, Mrs. Engelhardt. Of course not. I would never do that," and Mrs. Engelhardt said, incensed, "Well! I should hope not! That would be highly unethical."

Haltingly, as if Essie Spivak were close beside her, nudging her in the ribs, Katya tried to explain that her mother had called because there was an "emergency situation" — money was needed for medical care — but Mrs. Engelhardt stared at her without evident sympathy and did not speak. Katya said, "I have some money saved. I would need to borrow only two hundred thirty dollars — from my salary, I mean — for the next two or three weeks," and Mrs. Engelhardt said coolly, "'Only' two hundred thirty dollars! Katya, your salary is one hundred eighty-two a week before taxes and other deductions. This is well above the minimum-wage guidelines for minors, and we provide you with what we believe to be quite generous room and board here, as one of our family practically. No, Katya, borrowing from your future salary is not feasible. I know exactly what Max would say: 'What if she quits? We're hardly likely to sue a nanny for unearned wages.' That's how Max is, Katya. So I'm sorry. But borrowing such a sum of money at your age is not a good idea in any case, and I'm surprised that your mother would ask such a favor of me — she has never even met me — and of you, a minor. Your mother must have many other sources to borrow from, I would think — relatives? neighbors? I'm sure you understand and that this was not your idea, Katya." And so Katya had no choice but to smile numbly: "I guess so, Mrs. Engelhardt. You are right. I'm sorry for asking . . ."

Katya went away shaken, shamed. A flash of disgust for both her mother and for smug Mrs. Engelhardt left her weak. A vision came to her of the showy split-level house on the channel bursting into flames . . . The Engelhardts would be trapped in their bedroom and could not escape. But the children would be trapped, too. And the Hispanic housekeeper. Not just the Engelhardts, whom she hated, but these innocent victims, too, and so Katya relented, the burning house vanished and was gone. And yet a cruel smile distended her face, which felt masklike, brittle. For such power lay within her if she wished to execute it.

She heard the death bell knelling.
And every stroke did seem to say,
Hardhearted Barbara Allen.

8

SHE CALLED THE MAGIC NUMBER. On the back of Mr. Kidder's card.

She had not thrown the little white card away. She'd kept the little white card, knowing it might be precious.

Thinking, *Momma would approve. Momma would be impressed!*

It was a shock to her that her mother had returned to Atlantic City, as she'd promised not to do; yet it was not truly a surprise. You did not want to inquire too closely into what Essie Spivak was doing in Atlantic City, but there was no doubt: the raw appeal in her voice, her fear, her terrible need, could not be mistaken. Katya smiled to think how, in Atlantic City, if you didn't have money yourself, the next best thing was to be connected with someone who did.

The phone rang. There came a woman's voice: "Hello. Kidder residence."

Katya had an impulse to hang up quickly. This would be the housekeeper, Mrs. Bee. But she said, "Mr. Kidder, please."

"And who shall I say is calling?"

"Katya."

A brief, chill pause. Invisible Mrs. Bee frowned. "Katya who?"

"Just Katya. Mr. Kidder expects me to call, and he will know who Katya is."

And this turned out to be so.

9

It was arranged: Katya would go that night to 17 Proxmire Street, to Mr. Kidder's studio at the rear of the house. She was not to ring the doorbell — "Mrs. Bee need not be involved, dear!" She was to go to Mr. Kidder at dusk — that is, as soon as she was free of her obligations to the Engelhardts, and free of their scrutiny. After the children were safely in bed for the night.

Nearly 11 P.M. when at last Katya slipped away from the Engelhardts' house, from her ground-floor room that opened onto New Liberty Street. In stealth she slipped away. There were lights in the Engelhardts' bedroom, but they would have no idea that their hired girl was gone from the house. Half walking, half running to Proxmire Street, thinking with a thrill of dread, *No one will know where I am. Except Marcus Kidder.*

On the phone, he'd been immediately sympathetic. Katya had told him it was a "family emergency," a "medical emergency," and there was a tremor in her voice he could not have doubted.

At this hour Proxmire Street was quiet, mostly darkened. Behind the ten-foot privet hedge the large old oceanside houses of the wealthy were near-invisible. At 17 Proxmire, Katya hesitated before pushing open the wrought-iron gate. Almost she wished the gate might be locked: she would turn away then, and go back to the ground-floor nanny's room. But the gate swung open at her touch, for it was a gate that was never locked. *He will help me*, Katya thought. Her heart beat wildly in anticipation.

Here, so close to the ocean, the air was balmy and windy and smelled of rain. The large shingleboard house loomed up before Katya like a great sail-ship becalmed on land. Most of the house appeared to be dark; only a wan light glowed at the rear. Katya followed the flagstone path toward the front stoop and then walked through the thick damp grass to the rear. How quiet it was! If someone saw her! In Bayhead Harbor there were security patrols, local police in squad cars cruising Ocean Avenue and the secluded tree-lined streets of the wealthy. If Katya were sighted making her way through the grass like this . . . But no one saw, no one stopped her. At the rear of the house she saw Mr. Kidder in the lighted room, standing at a rear door looking out. At once the scene was comforting to her: a secret place, a haven. On the flagstone terrace where they'd had "tea-time," an outdoor light shone. There was no moon; the sky was oppressive and opaque. The ocean, which should have been visible on the far side of the dunes, had vanished, except for the heavy sullen *slap-slap-slap* of the surf. Katya hesitated, feeling a strange thrill of excitement, seeing white-haired Mr. Kidder another time before he was aware of her.

She liked it that he was so tall. That he carried himself with dignity. From this distance he was a handsome man, you would think: you could not see the fine creases and lines in his skin. And how thoughtful he looked, standing in the doorway. When Katya stepped forward breathlessly into the light, Mr. Kidder was roused from his dreamy mood, came quickly to seize her by the hands and draw her into the house with him. "Dear Katya! You've come."

Warmth lifted from his skin. There was a fragrant scent of cologne, a smell of something tartly sweet on his breath as he stooped to brush his lips against her cheek.

Katya stiffened involuntarily. This was not a kiss exactly — was it? In her agitated state, she did not want to be touched.

The studio was as Katya recalled it from her first visit: the lattice windows, crowded bookshelves, brightly colored sofa and chairs. On the walls, Mr. Kidder's portraits; in vases, glittering and gleaming like sparks of fire, Mr. Kidder's fossil flowers. At

[56]

night, by lamplight, the space looked larger, more mysterious; the artist's easel and art things were obscured in shadow in a far corner. There was the smell of paint and turpentine, which made Katya's nostrils pinch.

A private room; no one would intrude. Mrs. Bee had very likely gone to bed.

"Dear Katya! You sounded so upset on the phone. Some sort of family emergency — what is it?"

Katya had prepared a story of medical bills, hospital bills, health problems, but as Mr. Kidder regarded her with his sympathetic blue gaze, the admonition came to her: *Can't lie to this man! He sees into my heart.* "My mother owes someone money. She's in Atlantic City. I hadn't known that. She's terrified. She asked me to borrow money from Mrs. Engelhardt, but Mrs. Engelhardt refused. My mother used to work at a casino in Atlantic City — she was a blackjack dealer. That's where she met my father. Sometimes I hate her, Mr. Kidder, I wish she would die! Then I'm so afraid for her, that something will happen to her and she *will* die. She needs three hundred dollars right away, and I have seventy dollars saved, so I only need to borrow . . ." In dismay Katya heard her voice, faltering, flat, the nasal Jersey accent that rendered even these heartfelt words unconvincing as if fabricated — and yet she was telling the truth.

Mr. Kidder listened gravely. As Katya continued to speak, words spilling from her, angry half-sobs, quietly Mr. Kidder went to a desk, took up a checkbook, and asked her to spell out her mother's name. The check was for three hundred dollars.

Three hundred! Katya had asked for less.

With childlike gratitude she squeezed his hand and leaned on her toes to brush her lips against the man's dry, just perceptibly wrinkled cheek. "Mr. Kidder, thank you! You are so — so wonderful! I will pay this back, I promise. I will pay it back with interest."

Mr. Kidder laughed, pleased. He indicated that Katya should sit down. "I'm sure you will, Katya. In time."

Now she had the check, a slip of paper magically containing the wholly unlike names Esther Spivak and Marcus C. Kidder, Katya would have liked to leave. But how could she say no to Mr. Kidder's hospitality after he'd been so kind to her? She could not.

She sat on a sofa with chintz-covered pillows. She supposed that Mr. Kidder would offer her something to drink — he'd been drinking wine, she guessed — but instead he sat facing her, somewhat distractedly, in a straight-backed chair; he leaned forward, elbows on his knees. He was wearing an expensive-looking linen shirt in a pale lavender shade, and dark purple summer trousers with a sharp crease. Katya did not want to think that the white-haired old gentleman had changed his clothes, combed his hair, and shaved, just for her. (Maybe he'd had other guests at the house earlier? Maybe he'd gone out with friends?) In the warm lamplight Katya could see the crinkled skin beside Mr. Kidder's eyes, from so many years of smiling; she could see stray wire-like white hairs protruding from his eyebrows and from his ears. Katya smiled, thinking, *Those hairs would tickle!* and Mr. Kidder asked what she was smiling at, and Katya blushed and said she didn't know.

"Maybe you're happy, Katya? That's reason enough."

Katya agreed, it was.

"You are a happy person, I think? You seem to have the gift of joy." Mr. Kidder spoke lightly, as if "gift of joy" had quotation marks around it. "Except for your concern for your mother, which is altogether natural."

Katya agreed, it was.

"Or are you just agreeing with me, eccentric old Marcus Kidder, in order to be, like any clever child, agreeable?"

Katya laughed, blushing. The check was in her straw bag and the straw bag on her knees, and in a fleeting fantasy she saw herself raising both elbows, employing her sharp elbows like weapons if Mr. Kidder moved toward her.

But this was a shameful thought, and a ridiculous thought: Mr. Kidder was not that sort of man, you could tell.

"Do you believe in soul mates, Katya? That some individuals are fated for each other? No matter the differences between them. No matter the vagaries of external circumstance."

Vagaries. The word made Katya uneasy; she wasn't sure of its meaning. But *soul mate* she guessed she understood.

From a nearby table Mr. Kidder had taken up an artist's sketchbook, to show her a drawing in pastel chalk, which made Katya laugh in surprise. "Mr. Kidder, is that *me?*" For the softly muted, feathery drawing was of a girl who resembled Katya enough to be a sister, with the Spivak family cheekbones, the set of Katya's eyes, the slant of her eyebrows and the shape of her nose . . .

"This is Katya-in-memory, not you," Mr. Kidder said, with mild disdain for the drawing, though Katya thought it was amazing, wonderful: her, and yet not her, a younger, softer-featured, prettier, and surely nicer Katya Spivak. "Now that you are here, my vision seated before me, I see exactly where I went wrong. May I — ?" Mr. Kidder tore the sketch out of the book and to Katya's dismay crumpled it in his fist as if it were of no worth. He took up a stick of chalk and began sketching, peering at Katya as if taking her measure. "If you aren't tired, Katya, and don't mind posing for me. For just a few minutes."

Katya was uneasy. She had not expected this. Yet telling herself, *How can I say no? Mr. Kidder has been so kind.*

And so Katya posed for the first time for Marcus Kidder. Self-conscious, unsure what to do with her hands. She wet her lips nervously. She felt a sudden itch in her right armpit that she couldn't dare scratch. Mr. Kidder asked her to turn her head toward the light, to lift her shoulders and lean forward, to cross her legs at the ankles, uncross her legs, again cross her legs at the knees . . . Over her T-shirt and shorts she was wearing a loose-fitting white terrycloth pullover, which Mr. Kidder asked her to remove, which she did. Yet still something wasn't right. "Too much shadow is being cast onto your face. Come here, Katya — this will be much better." Mr. Kidder switched on lights at the rear of the studio, dragged over a wooden stool with a back and arms of about the height of a baby's highchair for Katya to sit in. He stood at the easel, more comfortable there, and began rapidly sketching, pausing from time to time to adjust Katya's arms, legs, shoulder, head, as if she were a mannequin; he asked her to remove her hair from her ponytail, which she did. "Ah! Such lovely hair, it seems cruel to disguise."

By degrees Katya began to feel less self-conscious. This was flattering — wasn't it? How many girls, how many women in Vineland, had ever posed for an actual artist? Katya smiled to think how she would show her portrait to her sisters and to her mother; just possibly to Roy Mraz, who might not laugh at her but be impressed. *This rich guy. In Bayhead Harbor, right on the ocean . . .*

Mr. Kidder was saying that he'd known from the first, seeing Katya on Ocean Avenue, that there was something special in her, and something special between them; in the course of a life, there are not really many mysteries, not mysteries you would call profound, but he had no doubt that this was one of them: "The link between us. Which isn't yet evident. But will emerge, I think — like a glass flower taking shape, molten glass at first and then shaped, completed."

Vaguely Katya nodded, though she wasn't sure that she understood; she did feel, she supposed, some sort of rapport with this man that she'd never quite felt with any other older man, she guessed. Her father had been much younger when she'd last seen him . . .

Mr. Kidder paused, lightly chiding her: "Dear Katya! No melancholia, please. The gift of joy is my subject tonight."

Katya looked up, and Katya smiled. She could almost think that Mr. Kidder had the power to make her beautiful, if he drew her "beautiful." If Katya was beautiful, maybe her picture would be in the newspaper one day, or on TV; her father would see her, recognize her, and return to Vineland . . . *Stupid*, Katya thought. *You are such an asshole — just stop.*

Mr. Kidder told her that he was by nature a nocturnal being and wondered if Katya was, too, and Katya said yes, she'd always liked to stay up late past her bedtime and read, since she'd been a little girl. And sometimes she would sneak away — not even her sisters would know where she'd gone — out of the house and into a neighbor's old barn that hadn't been used for years but still smelled of hay, and of horses and cows . . . Mr. Kidder asked Katya what she liked to read, and Katya said any kind of book, from the public library in Vineland; when she had a book to read, she never felt lonely. Mr. Kidder asked her if at other times she felt lonely, and Katya said "Yes!" Yes, she did. Not meaning to speak so emotionally, but that was how it came out, for Mr. Kidder spoke so kindly to her, Katya was drawn to say more than she meant. And Mr. Kidder paused in his sketching, saying that that was true for him, too: "The more people you know, like me, the vast network of relatives, old, dear friends, business associates — ah, so many of these! — for Marcus Cullen Kidder is, among myriad other identities, a trust-fund child — shamelessly so, at this advanced age yet a child — the lonelier you are."

Such a twisty speech, like a pretzel: Katya had to laugh. Mr. Kidder was like no one she knew, both eloquent and comical. He was the most intelligent person she'd ever met, far more intelligent than any of her teachers at Vineland H.S., and yet he was so playful, like someone on TV. Behind the easel he did a kind of shuffle-dance and made a snorting noise with his lips. Katya felt inspired to say, "Mr. Kidder, that can't be right. Anyone would think that a person who lives in a house like this right on the ocean and has a famous name everyone in Bayhead Harbor knows would never be lonely," and Mr. Kidder made the snorting noise again, saying, "'Anyone' is a blockhead."

Blockhead! Katya had never heard this word before. It made her laugh.

"I think you're being silly, Mr. Kidder. Like Funny Bunny. You make things up to worry over, then believe them."

"Do I!" Mr. Kidder paused in his sketching to regard Katya with thoughtful eyes. "But Funny Bunny is cuddly, eh? As his creator, M.K., is not."

To this Katya made no reply.

A *fair maiden*, he'd called her. That other time. When he'd played that beautiful song, "Barbara Allen," for her. Saying she made him think of — what was it? — *heimweh*, homesickness. She had not understood; she'd have liked to ask but dared not.

He'd spoken of a special mission for Katya. Not to be revealed quite yet. Handsomely rewarded . . .

As if Mr. Kidder could read her thoughts and did not wish to acknowledge them, briskly he told her to "relax, please" — to turn her shoulders just slightly to the left and brush her hair out of her eyes: "We need to see those beautiful if over-wary eyes, dear!" Positioning herself at a new angle, Katya could now see several of the portraits on the wall: women and girls so rendered by the artist's graceful brushstrokes as to bear a family resemblance, especially in their smiles, which were similarly sweet, hopeful. Katya had no way of knowing if Mr. Kidder's subjects really did resemble one another or whether this was the way the portraitist saw them, or wished to see them. Not one of the subjects was less than attractive, and yet not one was glamorous like the women in the framed photographs in Mr. Kidder's music room. Here was a more innocent sort of female beauty, as the ages of the subjects appeared to be generally younger. Katya was most struck by a girl of her approximate age, with pale blond hair arranged in a classically smooth old-fashioned pageboy, and an ethereally delicate face; the girl's eyes were hazel, made to glow with light by the artist's touch, as if alive. Around her slender neck she wore a dark velvet ribbon affixed by a pearl pin. In the bottom right-hand corner of the portrait was NAOMI 1956.

"That girl, Naomi — who is she?" Katya asked, and Mr. Kidder said, frowning, "No one. Now." It was a blunt statement that made Katya uneasy. References to Mr. Kidder's private life that weren't initiated by Mr. Kidder himself seemed to register with him as a kind of affront.

Whose business? None of your business. Katya knew: you can't push them too far. Adult men, and guys like Roy Mraz, who could turn mean without warning.

Thinking of Roy, Katya felt suddenly weak, faint. Rarely did she allow herself to think of her "distant cousin," knowing it would upset her. Yet a wave of longing came over her for Roy's rough hands, his mouth . . .

Jesus, Katya! Nobody's going to hurt you.

"Eyes here, please!" Gently Mr. Kidder chided Katya, who turned to him with a pained smile, trying not to squint though there was a piercing light from a high-wattage bulb in her eyes like a sliver of glass.

As if Mr. Kidder had known where Katya's thoughts had drifted, he became distracted, disappointed with what he'd sketched. "Damn!" He crumpled the portrait he'd been sketching in his fist, tossed it onto the floor; Katya winced as if he'd hit her. Yet did this mean the session was ending? And she could leave? Katya noticed that his forehead was oily with perspiration and his breath was sounding husky, as if there might be something clogged in his sinuses or in his chest. Mr. Kidder wiped his face with a handkerchief, turned aside to press the heel of his hand against his chest, as if to mitigate pain; Katya had seen one of her elderly Spivak relatives make a similar gesture, standing apart from the others at a family gathering. But Mr. Kidder quickly recovered. It did not seem that truly there was anything wrong with Marcus Kidder, who made it a point to stand so straight and to speak so forcibly to his model. Asking her now if she'd like a little break and something to drink — "If, discreetly, I dilute it with

[63]

sparkling water, a half-glass of wine?" — but before Katya could accept the offer, quickly Mr. Kidder said, "Better not, Katya! Not tonight." He went away and returned with a tall, fizzing glass of what appeared to be club soda for Katya, with a twist of lemon, and for himself a glass of dark red wine.

"Wine might put you to sleep, Katya. We'll save wine for another time."

Another time. So this modeling session hadn't been a failure, Mr. Kidder would want her back.

Thirstily Katya drank the club soda. Her mouth felt parched. It was true she'd become sleepy, as if hypnotized. *What if he has put something in this?* passed through her mind, but the thought was too fleeting to be retained.

Another time gave her hope. Maybe a modeling career? What would the Spivaks think — how impressed would Katya's sisters be? And what would Roy Mraz think — Katya Spivak, whom he'd so taken for granted, an actual *model* . . .

"Just a few more minutes, dear. We've been at an impasse — there is something clouding your mind, but I think we can banish it if we try. You are such an attractive young woman, Katya — you must tell yourself, *I am Katya, I am very special, I am me.* Truly, you mustn't laugh!" for Katya had begun to laugh, embarrassed. "I forbid my models to laugh, under pain of banishment." So Mr. Kidder spoke cajolingly, to soothe her, and began again sketching her, in a more playful mood, with rapid, deft strokes of his chalk. "Tell me, dear, how do you like working for the Mayflies?" — Mr. Kidder's comical name for the Engelhardts; and Katya laughed, but said yes, she liked working for them, because she liked the children and the housekeeper, Maria, was nice to her, and of course there was Bayhead Harbor, nothing like spending the summer in Vineland, where it was so damned hot. She told Mr. Kidder that sometimes she didn't feel comfortable in the Engelhardts' house, where Mrs. Engelhardt was suspicious of her, always finding fault, saying that Katya was a good nanny but then

[64]

turning around and criticizing her, and from Maria she'd learned that Mrs. Engelhardt had hired and fired nannies in the past, and it was hard for her now to hire anyone who knew her. Mr. Kidder listened gravely to this and asked if Mrs. Engelhardt had actually threatened to fire Katya, and Katya hesitated and might have lied, but seated facing the artist, only a few feet away, and knowing how Mr. Kidder could read her thoughts, she said, "N-no, Mr. Kidder. Not yet."

"Mrs. Mayfly disapproves of little Katya staying out late, eh? Is that it?"

"No! Mrs. Engelhardt hasn't a clue that I'm not in bed."

Mr. Kidder behind the easel continued to sketch Katya in quick inspired strokes, as if he hadn't heard this boastful remark. He said, "Because it would be tragic, dear, if you were sent away from Bayhead Harbor. Before we have time to become properly acquainted."

Tragic! Katya had to smile at *tragic.* A big, ungainly word not common in Vineland, New Jersey.

Mr. Kidder ceased speaking to Katya, and Katya's eyelids began to droop. She fumbled to set down the glass of club soda, and in silence the artist continued with his sketching. How abstracted he seemed, utterly absorbed. *So long as Mr. Kidder sees me, I am safe.*

It had been a childish fantasy of Katya's that her father might be watching her from somewhere close by. Jude Spivak had disappeared one day from Vineland "in debt" — thousands of dollars, Katya had heard. And how scary the words *in debt* were, as if Katya's father were stuck in something like the soft black smothering muck of the Pine Barrens after a heavy rain. Jude Spivak hadn't left his wife and family with a hasty wet kiss for nine-year-old Katya and the careless promise *Daddy will be back for your birthday, you bet!* Instead, Katya liked to imagine that Daddy was watching her. He was watching over her. Maybe he was a trucker. So many trucks came through Vineland on Route 55, and it wasn't far-fetched to think that Jude Spivak might be driving one of these. And maybe Jude Spivak had kept contact with certain of his relatives, for he'd been close to his brothers and cousins; maybe he came to see them in secret. And so maybe he'd been watching Katya over the years. Seeing that she was a good girl, or tried to be a good girl. Seeing that she was good-looking, sexy; boys were attracted to her, and even men. If Katya became really beautiful, Daddy would be impressed and come to claim her. When Katya had confessed something of this fantasy to her sister Lisle, Lisle had said bluntly, *Wouldn't bet on that, Katya.*

What these words meant, Katya hadn't wanted to know.

"Katya! Wake up, dear."

Marcus Kidder was hovering over Katya, trying not to sound agitated. As if he'd made some sort of blunder that had to be made right, and quickly. "I've exhausted my model, I'm afraid. And the hour has become unwittingly late — I mean, I have unwittingly allowed the hour to become late. I will drive you to the Mayfly residence immediately." The Mayfly joke fell flat, Mr. Kidder spoke so lamely.

But Katya was awake now, and on her feet. Just slightly groggy, shaking her head. But in a minute she had revived. "No, thank you, Mr. Kidder! I can walk."

How airless it seemed in Mr. Kidder's studio suddenly. Katya was eager to leave. Snatched up her straw bag, and at the door before Mr. Kidder could protest: "Katya, please. You must let me drive you home — it's the least I can do. My driver isn't on duty at the moment, but I am a fully licensed and fully capable driver, I promise." But Katya, in an excitable mood, insisted she wanted to walk and fended the old man off, saying she was stiff from sitting so long and wanted to walk: "But thanks for the check, and Momma thanks you, too." For the check was safely in Katya's bag, and that was the crucial thing.

Yet Mr. Kidder would not let Katya go just yet. It was like leaving the home of an elderly relative, a female relative, who has to retain you for a few minutes, pull at your hands, kiss you; so in the doorway Marcus Kidder, who'd been so assured during the modeling session, was flustered and agitated now, for no reason Katya could understand. He took hold of her shoulders as if to embrace her or to kiss her. Katya stood very still, not wanting to ease away from him, smelling his wine breath and that odor of slightly stale cologne. Thinking, *Mr. Kidder is my friend, Mr. Kidder would never hurt me. Mr. Kidder will help me.* In his warm, dry hands, Mr. Kidder framed Katya's face. She could feel these hands tremble, and she could feel Mr. Kidder's excitement. How eager she was to be gone from this room. Her heart was beating in mild revulsion from the man's touch, but Katya forced herself to remain still, politely unresisting. In Mr. Kidder's eyes, which brimmed with moisture, Katya saw such tenderness for her, such desire, or love, she felt that her throat might close, she might begin to cry. Gravely Mr. Kidder lowered his face to hers. Katya held her breath, but he just brushed his lips against her forehead and did not try to kiss her on the mouth.

"Katya, goodnight! Next time, soon, we will plan for a longer visit."

10

NEXT MORNING BY SPECIAL DELIVERY she sent the check to her mother: Essie Spivak, c/o The Silverado Motel, 1677 Eleventh Street, Atlantic City, NJ. Hoping that her mother would not be suspicious of who Marcus C. Kidder was and why he was providing Katya with three hundred dollars to send to her.

She was excited, and she was relieved. She was hopeful. Thinking, *Now Momma will be safe! For a while.*

Thinking, *Now Momma will love me a little better.*

More reasonably thinking, as she watched three-year-old Tricia run and stumble, squealing with delight, on the sandy private beach of the Bayhead Harbor Yacht Club, *Maybe this will make a difference.*

And finally, *At least Momma will call me and thank me.*

11

IT BEGAN TO HAPPEN THEN. After the check for three hundred dollars, and after she'd posed for him. *Posed* so casually now a part of her vocabulary. *A fair maiden. Heimweh. Soul mate. Fated. Handsomely rewarded.* Waking from a dream of mysterious urgency in the chilly dark before dawn when seagulls cried outside her window, hearing his voice as intimately as if he'd been lying beside her: *Katya, my dear.*

It began to happen then, that she thought of him often. At first quizzically, even derisively, and then with an inexplicable and powerful yearning. The old nagging thoughts of her mother and of her lost father and of her home on County Line Road in Vineland and of Roy Mraz were thunderhead clouds, sultry with rain, but her thoughts of Marcus Kidder were high-scudding, fleecy white clouds gently blown across a fair, clear, washed-looking sky and made you smile to see them. *A longer visit*, he'd said. *Next time.* Her canny Spivak instinct told her, *I don't think so, old man!* and yet the fact was, Marcus Kidder had been kinder to Katya Spivak, more generous and more caring, than anyone outside her immediate family had ever been. Of course she knew, or believed that she knew, that Marcus Kidder was attracted to her — that sick-melting look in his eyes — and yet she did not think it was a crude sexual attraction. He wanted to help her, he wanted to protect her. She'd been singled out by him on Ocean Avenue, he'd said. And so Katya was singular, and special. This was a secret she might bear, like the secret tattoo, a smudged, inky black, clumsily executed, inch-high spade shape on the soft flesh of the inside of her right thigh that Roy Mraz had wanted for her.

And he's rich . . .

So she would boast to Roy, to make him jealous. So she would boast to her mother and to her sisters, to make them jealous. *See? I don't need just you.*

Thinking of him during the long nanny day. Predawn, early morning, and midmorning, lunchtime and early afternoon, afternoon and early evening, exhaustion and bed. Being scolded by Mrs. Engelhardt — "Katya, where are you and Tricia? We're late" — and being stared at by Mr. Engelhardt when she wore her two-piece swimsuit at the yacht club beach or on Mr. Engelhardt's gleaming white yacht. When she was bathing the baby, such a compact, fat little gurgling-mouthed baby with shiny eyes, powerful lungs when he chose to scream but at other times wonderfully docile, a happy-seeming baby, with an amazing strong grip of his tiny fingers on Katya's single forefinger so she was provoked to think, *It must be meant for me, that I will have a baby of my own,* and somehow Mr. Kidder was involved in this revelation, for he saw in her such goodness, such a special soul, it was right and good that such a special soul should have a baby, or babies. She thought of him when she was with Tricia, sprinting with the eager little girl along the beach, helping her feed the geese at the park, bathing her, putting her to bed; especially when she was reading to Tricia from *Funny Bunny's Birthday Party*, moving her fingers beneath the words at the bottom of the page, which by now Tricia had memorized. At such times Katya could feel Mr. Kidder's presence in the room.

Katya and Tricia had begun drawing Funny Bunny themselves, appropriating Mr. Kidder's comical white bunny in fanciful stories of their own. Katya quite enjoyed these sessions with the little girl, far more than she enjoyed hauling the Engelhardt children around in their mother's company. It was such fun drawing animals that walked upright like people but were much nicer than most people, who could have comical adventures that were resolved in a happy ending. As a little girl Katya had liked to draw, and then in middle school she'd become distracted by other things. It was like a neighbor's horse, Black Pete, a slouch-backed, good-natured horse kept in a pasture down the road that Katya had visited and petted at least once, sometimes twice a day; and then, in middle school, by degrees she'd ceased petting Black Pete and feeding him apples; over a winter she'd forgotten him, and then one day in the spring, driving with her mother, she saw the empty pasture and said, "Where's Black Pete?" and Katya's mother said, "That old horse you used to pet? It's been gone for months." Katya's mother cast her a sidelong look, squinting through a cloud of exhaled smoke, as Katya sat in stunned silence, biting her lower lip. *Don't ask,* she thought. She could not bear to learn what had happened to her old friend Black Pete.

Black Pete's Birthday Party: this could be the title of Katya Spivak's book for children?

And she began to see his name. Began to be conscious of seeing his name in unexpected places. Pushing the baby in his stroller, clutching at Tricia's moist little hand as they entered Harbor Park on their excursion to feed the geese, and there on the right was a Victorian-style pavilion to which Katya had never given more than a glance before: KIDDER MEMORIAL PAVILION. (When they'd entered the park that morning with Marcus Kidder, he'd said nothing about the pavilion, out of modesty — or indifference.) Another day she happened to see, on Charity Street, which intersected with Ocean Avenue, a dignified old brick townhouse bearing a bronze plaque: HENDRICKS, STAPLES, MANNHEIMER & KIDDER INVESTMENTS. (But this Kidder could not be Marcus, Katya thought. Must've been a younger relative.) And there was the Bayhead public library, which bore the full name Bayhead Harbor Kidder Memorial Library, in a historic gray shingleboard house to which numerous wings had been added over the decades. Katya loved this little library, just to enter the front door, to hear the hardwood floor creak just perceptibly beneath her feet, to smell the rich old-library smells. In the children's room there was a display of local authors, and predominant here were several picture books by Marcus C. Kidder, including *Funny Bunny.* "Look, Tricia!" Katya said, pointing. "There's *Funny Bunny.*"

The little girl stared, sucking at a finger. How had her special book from Mr. Kidder come to be here?

Katya was intrigued to see that there were three other children's books by Marcus C. Kidder as author and illustrator: *Duncan Skunk's First Day at School, The Little Leopard Who Changed His Spots,* and *Elgar the Flying Elephant.* Tricia clamored for these books, which Katya checked out of the library, using Mrs. Engelhardt's card. "This author — Marcus Kidder — lives in Bayhead Harbor, I guess?" Katya asked the librarian, a middle-aged woman with red harlequin glasses and a cordial smile, who said, "Mr. Kidder certainly does! He's our most generous donor. He used to come in here all the time, but we haven't seen much of him lately." Katya asked who the Kidders were and was told that they were an "old, distinguished family" who lived in New York City and spent summers in Bayhead Harbor. "The older generation has died out — now there's mostly just Mr. Kidder. If he has young relatives, we don't see them in Bayhead. Mr. Kidder is on our board of trustees, and he's on the board of the Historic Society, which keeps up the Bayhead Lighthouse. He's a musician, too, and a composer — there've been evenings in the park where music of his was performed . . ." The woman spoke so warmly of Marcus Kidder, yet with an air of regret, or longing, that you could see she'd have liked Mr. Kidder to be her friend, but that hadn't happened. Trying not to sound overcurious, Katya asked her how many books Mr. Kidder had written, and the librarian said, "That I know of, just these. Four children's books." Katya checked the publication dates, which ranged from 1955 to 1962. *Funny Bunny* had been published in 1961. So long ago! "Mr. Kidder didn't write anything after this?" Katya asked, and now the librarian squinted at her through the red-framed harlequin glasses, not smiling so cordially now: "No. I don't think he did." Katya heard herself asking, "Why not?" and the librarian said coolly, as if Katya were an outsider prying into a private local matter, "I really don't know. Why don't you ask him yourself?" The remark was intended to be dismissive, but Katya said, clutching the books to her chest, "I might just do that."

That evening, when Katya opened *Duncan Skunk's First Day at School* to read to Tricia at her bedtime, she discovered the dedication: *To My Lost Naomi (1939–1956).*

The girl in the portrait: Naomi. Young, possibly younger than Katya, with wavy blond hair, a smile to break your heart, large hazel eyes rendered by the artist beautiful but, Katya had thought, vacant. The smile was sweetly hopeful; here was a girl eager to please. Or so the artist had rendered her. Around her neck was a dark velvet ribbon affixed with a pearl pin. The lost Naomi was prettier than Katya Spivak, for it was clear that she was much nicer, and richer. Certainly she was richer! Maybe she'd even been a Kidder, bound to Marcus Kidder by blood. The cruel thought came to Katya: *But Naomi is dead, and I am alive.*

12

WAITING FOR HER MOTHER to call. *Why, Katya, thank you! You have saved my life, honey . . .* She was excited and she was apprehensive and she was cunningly rehearsing what she would say when her mother asked who this Marcus C. Kidder was who'd been such a friend, who'd lent a stranger three hundred dollars. But her mother didn't call, and so didn't thank Katya. And didn't interrogate her about Mr. Kidder.

And when Katya called home, there was no answer, not even the familiar recording of Essie Spivak's bemused nasal voice: *Sorry, Essie must not be here or she'd take this call so please leave a message at the sound of the beep.* Instead the phone rang, rang in what must have been an empty house. When Katya called her sister Lisle, there was at least a recorded message, but Lisle never called Katya back, and so Katya called her other sister, Tracey, whose U.S. Army sergeant husband was stationed in Fort Dix, fifty miles north of Vineland. This older sister had never seemed to care much for Katya, for no reason Katya could guess, and said flatly to her, as soon as she heard Katya's hesitant voice, "If it's Mom you're calling me about, tell her no."

Katya asked, *No what?* and Tracey said, raising her voice to be heard over a shrieking child, "No, I will not lend that woman any more money. She owes Dwight and me six hundred dollars she promised she would repay, with interest back in June, and we haven't heard from her since, and can't get hold of her, and Lisle says she's drinking again, and probably using, living with some guy in Atlantic City, and Dwight says, 'That's it,' and I am in one hundred percent agreement. So, *no.*"

Meekly Katya apologized, and hung up.

13

SHE WOULD TELL HIM, *Sure it hurts — my mother never called. My sister never asked about me at Bayhead Harbor living with a rich family where I am a hired girl, a nanny. Where I do as my employers instruct, with a smile.*

And he would say, stroking her cheek, that melting-love look in his icy blue eyes, *But what a beautiful smile, Katya! My beautiful girl.*

PART II

14

This building will now be evacuated. This building will now be evacuated. At once . . .

She was eleven years old. She was in sixth grade at Vineland Middle School South. She was in her third-period class, which was social studies, when with no warning a harried voice was broadcast over the speaker system and you could see that the announcement was a surprise and a shock to Mrs. Wilnik, who was their teacher. And so stunned, somber Mrs. Wilnik, trying to remain calm, lifted her quavering voice and instructed the class to stand at their desks, row by row, in an orderly fashion, and to leave the room single-file, as in a fire drill, and walk — *walk, not run* — to the stairs and down the stairs and outside. Remember: *walk, not run.* And Katya was frightened, and Katya was excited, on her feet and buoyed along with the others, into the hall, so strangely crowded, like the inside of a tunnel or a sewer, to the stairs, which creaked beneath the combined weight of their many anxious feet, and plunging down the stairs single-file in an unnatural hush interrupted by the repeated amplified instructions in that harried deafening adult voice. Katya was quick as an eel — she was always quick, pushy, and cunning in such confused circumstances. She pushed forward to walk with a friend, the girls clutching at each other's chill hands in a thrill of panic — *A bomb? Think it's a bomb?* — for always at such times you want something to happen and the fear is — what? This was not a routine fire drill; there was no clanging alarm, and adult faces were grim, strained. *They don't know any more than we do* came the realization, and it was not a realization to give comfort. In this season of public school disturbances across the country, there had been shootings, bomb threats, and bombs, and in Paramus, New Jersey, earlier in the month there'd been a bomb threat and an actual bomb discovered in a student locker, which had failed to detonate. And so the older guys were nerved-up, sniggering and nudging one another in the ribs, running their hands over girls who squirmed from them, slapped at them like Katya amid the downward plunge on the stairs, through the opened doors, and outside onto the pavement . . .

Now they were outside, Katya and her classmates, being instructed, *Move away from the school building, move away from the school building, do not reenter the school building, move into the parking lot, away from the school building and into the parking lot in an orderly fashion,* but now they were running, pushing and colliding with one another, reassembling, breathless, exhilarated to see that Vineland volunteer firemen had arrived and were entering the school in bulky protective uniforms that gave them the exotic look of space travelers. There were Vineland police officers as well. There was Mr. Meer, the principal, speaking loudly, straining his voice to be heard over the din, ashen-faced and shaken as no one had ever seen him. Nothing is so frightening and nothing is so comical as adults in authority who are ashen-faced, visibly shaking. Teachers were speaking sharply, but no one was paying much attention now that they were outdoors. As soon as you are outdoors, as soon as the sky opens above you, the authority of adults shrinks. The authority of adults is revealed as puny, contemptible. It is possible to laugh at a man like Mr. Meer, who indoors, in the confinement of walls, ceiling, and floor, commands such authority, now forced to cup his hands to his mouth and shout to get attention. And not a tall man, it was revealed, not nearly so tall as the firemen in their exotic uniforms or the Vineland police officers. *You may go home,* Mr. Meer was telling them. *Classes are canceled for the remainder of the day. Do not reenter the school building, but in an orderly fashion you may leave the school property* . . . Was there a bomb threat? A bomb? It was being said that someone had called saying there was a bomb in the school wired to explode at noon. It was 11:48 A.M.

Katya was running with the others, away from the school building. She'd left her backpack beneath her desk in Mrs. Wilnik's classroom. And in her locker she'd left her raincoat. Though it was no longer raining; the sky was clear and the sun shone weirdly hot and overbright, as in one of those dreams in which everything is overbright and charged with a mysterious meaning. Katya left her friends milling about sharing cigarettes by the dumpster behind the 7-Eleven store, where often after school they gathered. She ran six, seven blocks to the Cumberland County Medical Clinic, where her mother supervised the cafeteria. For two years her mother had been working for the clinic, and in all that time she'd remained sober. Thinking, *Momma will be surprised to see me this time of day!* Thinking, *So she won't worry about me if she hears about the bomb.* But the food workers in the cafeteria told her that Essie Spivak wasn't working there any longer. Katya said yes, yes she was working there! She was the supervisor. Except now came a man with a shiny bald head and face and a sour smile who identified himself as the cafeteria supervisor, with the news, astonishing to Katya, that Essie Spivak hadn't been working at the clinic since March. But where was she? Katya asked, frightened, and the man said, with that pleased sour smile, he had no idea, but she wasn't here. Katya could not believe this. Her mother had been working at the Cumberland clinic for at least two years; often she told Katya and Lisle she felt good about herself, this was a good time in her life right now. Usually Katya's mother came home from work at about 7 P.M., sometimes later, five days a week; weekends, she sometimes worked a half-day. Or so Katya had believed. Her mother had not told anyone in the family that she'd quit the clinic or been fired, Katya was sure. Unless it was known and Katya had been shielded from the news: but why? Katya asked the sour-smiling

[81]

man why her mother wasn't working there any longer, and the sour-smiling man said, shrugging, "Ask her. She's your mother, isn't she?"

Dazed and shaken, Katya ran home. Ran through the house shouting, "Mom! Momma! Where are you!" though knowing that no one was there. Tracey had married the previous winter and moved away, and Katya's brothers, Dewayne and Ralph, had moved out. Only Lisle, who was a junior at Vineland High, remained at home, but she was often gone. In the kitchen in the refrigerator Katya found a Molson ale. Two ales she drank from the cans within forty minutes, sprawled on the sofa staring at MTV, and then she dozed off. She woke confused and frightened: it was dark in the living room, dark outside; there were voices in the kitchen. Katya's mother had been driven home by her man friend Artie, who'd been introduced to Katya and Lisle as a coworker of Essie's at the Cumberland clinic. Now Katya had to wonder who Artie was. Stumbling to her feet as her mother switched on the overhead light: "There was a bomb threat at school, but it didn't go off. I mean, the bomb didn't go off. They sent us home early." Katya spoke strangely; words seemed to tumble from her mouth. Her lips felt numb, rubbery. She was laughing at the expression of alarm, concern on her mother's face: "A bomb? Jesus."

Essie Spivak was in her early or mid-forties, and her skin was slightly coarse and her eyebrows too severely plucked, yet she was an attractive woman. She had dyed her graying hair dark cranberry red, which gave her an exotic, glamorous look. You'd expect her lipstick to be dark maroon, but it was a pale frosted pink-bronze that, thickly layered on her mouth, looked like an extra skin. She wore shoes with clattery heels and black designer jeans with glitter studs, a peach-colored designer blouse with a V neckline that exposed the tops of her creamy, shapely breasts. Her hips and belly were full, shapely. Her inch-long fingernails gleamed pink-bronze like her mouth and were filed with stylish blunt edges. She was smoking; she shifted her burning cigarette to her left hand and came to hug Katya with a sob of concern. "Jesus! Sweetie! A bomb! Thank God you're in one piece . . ." Stiffly Katya stood, feeling her mother's strong arms, her mother's breasts, which felt like balloons filled with warm water. It had been a long time since Katya's mother had hugged her. Katya's eyes filled with tears. These were involuntary tears; these were tears of outrage. Badly Katya wanted to push her mother away with her sharp elbows. Wanted to stab those balloon-breasts with her elbows. Yet badly Katya wanted to burrow into her mother's arms and cry, *You are a liar, you don't love me or any of us.* In the kitchen, someone was opening and shutting the refrigerator door. Must've been Momma's man friend, Artie, which might mean that Artie would be staying for supper with them or it might mean that Katya's mother was going out again, with Artie. And Katya could go with them, maybe. Katya shut her eyes, which were leaking tears, thinking, *Don't ask.*

15

"And you didn't ask her? Where she'd been all that time she'd led you to believe she was at work?"

"No. I never did."

Her answer was unexpected. Her answer was perverse. Mr. Kidder regarded her with sympathetic eyes. He'd been listening to her so attentively, as Katya spoke in a flat, bemused voice, relating this story she'd never told anyone else, even her sister Lisle; she was in danger of bursting into tears. And she did not want to burst into tears, not here. Not in Mr. Kidder's studio, as Mr. Kidder was sketching her portrait. Yet when someone is kind to you, you are most vulnerable. And there was such shame here, such petty shame. Katya knew that a man like Marcus Kidder had to pity her. Katya Spivak from Vineland, New Jersey, who was a hired girl here in Bayhead Harbor, a nanny living with the rich Engelhardts. She said, "I didn't ask my mother because I knew that she would have slapped my face, for 'spying' on her. And then she would know that I knew, but I would never know the truth anyway, because she wouldn't have told me."

It was Sunday afternoon, one of Katya's half-days off. She'd come to Mr. Kidder's studio to pose for him, at his request. And now Katya was crying, as she'd vowed not to. Hiding her warm flushed face in her hands. For she did not want Marcus Kidder, who believed that she was beautiful, to see that in fact she was ugly.

"Why, Katya. Please don't cry, dear." Laying down his pastel chalks, quickly stepping from the easel to come to her where she sat in her stiff pose, now hiding her face from him. He said,

"You may have been deceived by your mother, Katya, but I'm sure that she had her reasons for deceiving you. She didn't want to worry you, maybe. I'm sure that she cares for you very much. And please know that Marcus Kidder cares for you, too." It was the kindest thing anyone had ever said to Katya, and so gently uttered. It was not a statement that made a claim upon her, just a statement of fact. And Mr. Kidder embraced her, as you'd embrace a weeping child, to give comfort. And Katya held herself rigid at first, not wanting to be touched by the white-haired old man, for there was the faint fragrant smell of his cologne, and a drier smell of his skin, or his hair, that she did not like; a smell of his breath, a very slight smell, as of something dry and chalky, like the inside of a skull, which is desiccated and mere bone. Yet she was lightheaded, dazed, for no one had held her like this in a long time, no one had spoken so tenderly to her in a long time; and so Katya ceased resisting, slid her arms around Mr. Kidder, and hugged his lean body in return, hiding her warm weeping face in the crook of his neck.

"Dear Katya! No one will hurt you again."

16

"EYES HERE, KATYA! Your beautiful eyes."

It was early August. Following an overnight squall, the Jersey coast was littered with seaweed, sea kelp, rotting fish, and hundreds — thousands? — of jellyfish washed ashore half-alive, transparent tendrils quivering with venom. In Mr. Kidder's studio, Katya posed for the artist, seated in a straight-backed stool facing him at the easel a few feet away. It was then Mr. Kidder would tell her in the calmest, most matter-of-fact voice that he was a perfectionist in his art, if not in his life; he sought Katya's "perfect likeness," for it was a likeness he'd glimpsed many years ago, before he had seen Katya on Ocean Avenue.

Katya laughed uneasily. Was Mr. Kidder joking? Or was Mr. Kidder serious? He'd seated her so that she faced a sliver of light that seemed to pierce her very brain. She couldn't see the expression on Mr. Kidder's face.

Soul mates. At once you know. Born at the wrong times. One so old, the other so young . . .

What would her Vineland friends think of this? Katya wondered. Wanting to laugh — how they'd have reacted. *Some old guy hitting on Katya, disgusting old granddaddy, should be ashamed of himself.*

And then, maybe Katya loved him. Maybe.

For Marcus Kidder was so kind to her! Giving her so much money and never even asking if her mother had called her to thank her. (No. Essie Spivak had not called. Hadn't even acknowledged receiving the check, let alone expressed any curiosity about it. Their mother was "taking long weekends" in Atlantic City, Katya learned from her sister Lisle. At which casinos, and with whom: don't ask.)

How distant Katya felt from her family. The Spivaks were scattered like sea creatures washed ashore in the wake of a terrible storm, dazed and quivering with life, and some of this was a stinging, venomous life but the only life they knew. Katya thought, *I am not one of them! Not in Mr. Kidder's house.*

He would love her as her family could not, he seemed to promise. He would love her enough for two.

"Damn! Goddamn."

Sometimes he surprised her, losing his temper. While he was sketching Katya in pastel chalks, a sudden misstroke of the chalk and Mr. Kidder cursed, tore the paper in two, flung the chalk down so that it shattered on the floor.

Katya cringed, hoping he wasn't angry at her. Accustomed to men, boys and men, turning mean suddenly, blaming who's nearby.

"How elusive you are, Katya! A gossamer soul, like a butterfly's wings."

These pastel sketches were preliminary to paintings, Mr. Kidder told her. It was his intention to paint a sequence of oil portraits of her that would be "autonomous" artworks he'd envisioned long ago, before he'd actually seen her on Ocean Avenue.

"Before, even, you were born. I know this."

Marcus Kidder spoke quietly, forcefully. As his deft fingers moved, wielding chalk.

Skeptically, Katya asked how he knew this.

"Because, Katya, when I saw you there with those children, it was as if I remembered you. Except you'd been dressed differently that other time. Your hair had been loose, curlier. But it was you, Katya. You recognized me, too."

Katya tried to think: could this be so? A stranger, an older man with the most beautiful head of white hair, close beside her saying, *And what would you choose, if you had your wish?*

Mr. Kidder smiled at her from behind the easel. "Think back, dear! We both felt that we'd already met, in another lifetime perhaps. Somewhere."

Katya thought, *No! never.* This had to be a joke. Like Funny Bunny, who said such silly things, such far-fetched things, and expected you to believe them; and you had to love him, because he made you laugh.

Katya objected: if Mr. Kidder was going to tear up the sketches of her, why couldn't she have them? No one had ever drawn her likeness before — it didn't have to be perfect . . . But Mr. Kidder said, "No. When I achieve what I see, I will show you, and I will provide you with a copy. But it would pain me, Katya, for you to see anything less than perfection."

These other girls you've drawn, were they perfect? Katya wanted to ask but knew that Mr. Kidder would be offended by so personal a question.

And who was Naomi? And how did Naomi die?

No one had ever asked Katya Spivak what she planned to do with her life, but Marcus Kidder asked.

As Katya posed for him, so Katya spoke to him, shyly at first, for it seemed to her strange that Marcus Kidder should actually be interested in Katya Spivak's future; and then more openly, since he seemed sincere. So wonderfully sincere! Katya confided in the artist as she'd never confided in anyone: that she wanted to leave Vineland after high school, if she could; wanted to attend a good university, like Rutgers in New Brunswick, not the local community college. Mr. Kidder asked Katya what she'd like to study and Katya told him maybe psychology, linguistics — she'd seen a TV documentary about a team of psychologists who worked with chimpanzees, experimenting to determine if chimps could use language as human beings did. And more recently, since *Funny Bunny*, Katya was thinking she might study art and children's literature and become a children's book author/illustrator like Marcus Kidder . . .

"Really! But not 'like Marcus Kidder,' dear — there was only one of him."

Was this a rebuke? Was Mr. Kidder laughing at her? Yet next time Katya went to the studio, Mr. Kidder had a present for her: an artist's sketchpad and a box of colored pencils.

"Begin by sketching what you see. And don't get discouraged."

"Eyes here, Katya! That's my girl."

By the end of the forty-minute session Katya felt lightheaded. Her brain was fatigued as if she'd been high on ecstasy, sleepless through a night. Eyes aching from the effort of keeping them open and widened in the childlike way Mr. Kidder insisted on. *He is sucking my life from me,* came the warning thought, but too fleeting for Katya to grasp.

At the end of each session Mr. Kidder insisted upon walking Katya to the front gate. Speaking quietly to her as they made their way along the flagstone path in the semidark, his hand on her elbow gently guiding her, who needed no guiding, thanking her for her patience, and asking when she could come back again. At the front gate it was Mr. Kidder's custom to remove from his pocket, as if he'd only just thought of it, a clip of neatly folded bills, which he pressed into Katya's hand, provoking Katya to murmur, embarrassed, "Mr. Kidder, no — you don't have to pay me," though of course Katya expected to be paid, and was excited by the prospect of being paid; and Mr. Kidder laughed at her as you might laugh at a small child caught in a small lie. "Katya, of course I have to — you are precious to me, you know."

Truly she was embarrassed. Taking money like this, from Marcus Kidder. She shut her fingers over the bills without seeming to see what they were, or to acknowledge them, and kept her fingers shut tight until she was several blocks from 17 Proxmire Street, when she opened her hand and counted the money.

The first time he'd given her forty dollars. The second time fifty-five. The third time sixty-five dollars. So much money, for so little effort! *This money no one knows about. This money that is my secret. No taxes, and no deductions. Mrs. Engelhardt won't know. Momma won't know. All mine.*

17

In her swimsuit with a loose T-shirt over it and the wind whipping her hair, she was running — trying to run — on the beach at the yacht club in the wake of Tricia Engelhardt's waddling trot as the frothy, foamy, lead-colored surf washed up onto the beach, tickling and teasing the little girl's feet. Katya felt her bare feet begin to sink in the sand, soft dry sand that slowed her like a nightmare dream in which you run — try to run — but can't, cry for help — try to call for help — but can't. That day, humid hot even at the shore, Katya felt rivulets of sweat trickling down her sides. She was reliving Marcus Kidder's embrace. Oh God, she'd embraced Mr. Kidder without knowing what she'd done and a moment later stepped away, breathless and frightened, subtly revulsed and eager to escape him as he assured her, *Katya dear! I will pay you, of course.*

Underfoot, the fine white sand of the private beach was strewn with small broken shells, as if someone had deliberately tossed them there for another person to cut her bare feet on; overhead were shrieking herring gulls; on a desolate stretch of beach Katya suddenly saw her own body, naked, the swimsuit and the T-shirt torn from her, Katya Spivak's arms and legs outstretched in the coarse sand and her glassy eyes open to the sky as the hungry herring gulls swooped down . . .

There came a man's impatient voice: "Katya! For Christ's sake, watch where Tricia is headed, will you?"

Rudely wakened from her trance. Oh God, where was she? She'd allowed little Tricia Engelhardt to trot along the beach yards ahead of her — there was giggling little Tricia, about to stumble into a sinkhole. Katya screamed, "Tricia! Come here!" and managed to catch up with the child and swoop her into her arms just in time.

It was Mr. Engelhardt who'd shouted at Katya, from a board-walk through dune grasses, above the beach. Katya hadn't known that Tricia's father was anywhere close by. And there he stood, glowering at her, in swim trunks, an unbuttoned shirt, with a white yachting cap on his wiry graying hair. When Katya had first come to live in the Engelhardts' house, Mr. Engelhardt had gazed at her with a faint fond smile, and when his wife wasn't close by, he'd flirted openly with her. From time to time he'd tipped her — "No need for Lorraine to know, Katya. Just between you and me." Now Max Engelhardt's eyes moved on Katya crudely and without a trace of affection, and his tone was close to taunting: "Where the hell is your mind, Katya? On your boy-friend?"

Katya was shocked. Katya swallowed hard. Katya shielded her eyes against the sun. Katya was determined not to show this man the rage she felt toward him in that instant.

Saying, in a hurt voice, that she had no boyfriend . . .

"Good. And whoever he is, don't bring him into our house, ever."

18

"MRS. BEE! Here is my young artiste-friend Katya, visiting from Vineland, New Jersey."

Artiste-friend was Mr. Kidder's way of teasing. But Katya was made to feel flattered, too.

It was a warm, gusty August afternoon. Tea-time on the terrace behind Mr. Kidder's beautiful old shingleboard house. Mrs. Bee had prepared the meal, and Mrs. Bee served the meal. Mrs. Bee was a woman in her mid- or late fifties, in a grim dull gray housekeeper's uniform with white collar and cuffs, like something in a cartoon, exactly as Katya had imagined her: stout, short, puffy-faced, fussy and frowning and in love with gentlemanly Mr. Kidder, her longtime employer. For you never knew — certainly blushing Mrs. Bee never knew — if Mr. Kidder was kidding or serious, and if what he said about her — "busiest and best Mrs. Bee in all of Jersey" — was meant to be flattering or subtly mocking. It was clear to Katya that Mrs. Bee resented her: this blond young girl in such casual clothes, tank top, cutoffs, sandals, no one Mrs. Bee had ever seen before, yet an artiste-friend of Mr. Kidder's. Stiffly Mrs. Bee smiled as she served Katya and Mr. Kidder chilled cucumber soup, lobster and avocado salad, fresh-baked sourdough bread, casting a sidelong glance at Katya from narrowed pebble-colored eyes. *Don't think that I am impressed with you, like Mr. Kidder. I am not.*

What had been strange to Katya was how uninterested Mr. Kidder had been in talking about his children's books. *Funny Bunny, Elgar the Flying Elephant, The Little Leopard Who Changed His Spots, Duncan Skunk's First Day at School,* which

Tricia had loved, and Katya had loved also, wishing she'd had books like these when she'd been a little girl. But when Katya asked Mr. Kidder whether it was so, as the librarian had said, that he'd stopped writing and illustrating children's books, he'd stiffened and just shrugged; when Katya asked him why he'd stopped, when the books were so wonderful, he'd said coolly, "Children grow up and are gone. And so with adults." What this meant, Katya couldn't guess. She felt rebuffed, hurt. And Mr. Kidder relented, saying, "Katya, I'd done what I could in that vein. Each book was a replica of the preceding book, in an altered form. 'What I have done, I would not do again.'" Speaking wistfully, but in a way to suggest that the topic was closed.

Katya and Mr. Kidder were sitting side by side at the white wrought-iron table, looking toward the ocean, beyond a swelling of dunes, rippled dune grass. Katya could not stare hard enough at the rough, rolling waves of the Atlantic Ocean, froth like spittle, seabirds riding the crests of waves bobbing like white corks. How like vast sprawling nude figures, the sand dunes behind Mr. Kidder's property. Katya was thinking how strange it was that the ocean's waves never stop: Where do waves come from? And why? Something to do with the moon, she thought. Gravitational pull. She felt Mr. Kidder's fingers lightly on her bare forearm and tried not to be startled.

"To you, dear Katya! To your portrait, soon to be executed."

Sly Mr. Kidder had waited for Mrs. Bee to depart before lifting his glass of white wine in a toast, clicking it smartly against Katya's glass, which was in fact an elegant crystal wineglass like Mr. Kidder's, though filled with sparkling water and a twist of lime. Katya smiled her most dazzling smile, and drank.

Wanting to laugh at the prune-faced old bitch Mrs. Bee. What right had the woman to dislike Katya Spivak?

"Are you happy, Katya? I am."

"Yes, Mr. Kidder. I am."

The mouth speaks what the ear is to hear. What shrewd Old World wisdom, laced with cynicism. It had to have been one of Katya's Spivak grandparents who'd spoken in this way.

The mouth speaks to the ear: what I say is solely to manipulate whoever it is I am saying it to.

She would tell the old man what he wanted to hear. Why not?

Any man, any age. Max Engelhardt as well. Whatever they want to hear, the female instinct is to tell them.

So long as I am paid.

After the meal on the terrace they were to go inside to Mr. Kidder's studio, but today, as Mr. Kidder carefully explained, Katya was to "lie in repose" on the sofa, not sit in the chair. "The portraitist has enough preliminary sketches of the subject's head and shoulders," Mr. Kidder said. "Now the challenge is much greater — the subject's body."

Katya giggled nervously. "The subject — that's me, I guess?"

"Indeed yes, dear. You."

Inside Mr. Kidder's studio, Katya felt that something was different: but what? Must be the way the sofa had been repositioned. And the model's straight-backed stool was missing.

It was then that Mr. Kidder asked, as if he'd just thought of it, if Katya had a boyfriend. Pronouncing *boyfriend* in a bemused but neutral voice to suggest that Marcus Kidder wasn't a prurient old man hoping to pry into the sex life of a sixteen-year-old high school girl but only a friend, a concerned friend, with an interest in her private life.

Katya laughed. She felt blood rush into her face.

"D'you mean, Mr. Kidder, am I still a virgin? Or do I have sex with guys?" In Katya's flat south Jersey accent, the query was as jarring as a nudge in the ribs.

Mr. Kidder stared at her. Mr. Kidder began to cough. So taken by surprise, for a moment he couldn't speak.

Then, recovering, he leaned close to Katya to say, in a lowered voice, as if fearing Mrs. Bee might overhear: "But — have you been in love, Katya? Are you in love now? That should have been my question."

Reckless, Katya said, "Mr. Kidder, I don't know."

And then Katya was astounded. For there was Marcus Kidder instructing her: "Change into this, Katya. Just for tonight."

Holding out to her the red silk lingerie: lacy camisole with narrow straps, shimmery lace-trimmed panties. That Mr. Kidder had removed the lingerie from the Prim Rose Lane gift box and handed it to her so casually made the gesture all the more intimate, and insulting.

That damned old gift that Katya had hoped Mr. Kidder had forgotten.

Seeing Katya's look of shock, indignation, hurt, Mr. Kidder said, "It's the vivid color that makes this garment so alluring to the painter's eye. The silk texture, and the lace . . . Against your skin, Katya, the effect will be striking."

Katya pushed Mr. Kidder's hand away. Her face throbbed with heat. *No!* She would not.

Mr. Kidder smiled. *Yes!* He wanted this.

Katya insisted, *No!* She didn't want this. Stammering, "I — I never wear . . . underwear like that! Things like that are just to laugh at."

"No one will laugh, Katya. I can promise you that."

With a show of politeness, Marcus Kidder listened to Katya's protests as he went about the studio drawing blinds at the lattice windows, for much of the sky was still light from the waning evening sun, which seemed to expand at the horizon, an eerie luminous red. Next Mr. Kidder prepared the sofa for Katya to lie on, taking away the gaily colored pillows and replacing them with a black velvet cloth. Katya protested: *No! Damn it,* she was not going to wear that ridiculous underwear, clenching and unclenching her fists like an excited child. But Mr. Kidder took her fists and gently and forcibly opened them and placed the red silk lingerie in her hands firmly.

"Yes. You will change into this, Katya. No one will laugh."

So forcibly Mr. Kidder spoke, as one might speak to a recalcitrant child. Katya snatched the lingerie from him and stomped into the bathroom adjoining the studio to change.

"Damn him! I hate him."

How she resented this — resented him. Forcing her to do what she didn't want to do, because he wanted her to do it; addressing her in that voice of bemused superiority in which he addressed Mrs. Bee, which allowed for no contradiction. And so sullen, sulky Katya Spivak shed her clothes and put on the silk lingerie, dreading to see her reflection in the mirror.

When she returned to the studio, Mr. Kidder was busying himself at his easel and seemed to take no notice of her. Blushing fiercely, Katya arranged herself on the sofa, stiffly, trying not to glance down at her body in the scanty camisole and panties, which exposed so much of her small fleshy breasts, her belly, and her thighs. If she kept her knees pressed tightly together, she could hide from the artist's sharp eye the smudged little black spade tattoo on the inside of her left thigh, which Roy Mraz joked was his claim; she couldn't bear for Mr. Kidder to see it and to make a fuss over it, as he was sure to do.

"Beautiful Katya! Don't be self-conscious, dear. Beauty isn't a possession exclusively of the subject, but exists objectively in the world."

Katya muttered, "Bullshit."

But if she'd hoped to shock Marcus Kidder, she was disappointed: the artist just laughed.

A memory came to her, then. Her mother wore lingerie like this. Of course! Katya had forgotten.

Red silk, black silk, flesh-colored see-through bras, half-slips, camisoles and panties, wispy thongs, discovered one afternoon by

Katya and her sister Lisle when Katya was eleven and Lisle was fifteen, in their mother's bedroom bureau drawer. *Momma's boyfriend Artie gave her this,* Lisle said, holding a shortie black lace nightgown against her front, preening and smirking in the bureau mirror. *She'd be mad as hell if she knew we found it.*

Katya had examined a wispy black thong with a look of perplexed disgust. Was this some sort of panty? Who'd want to wear something so silly?

Lisle snatched the thong from Katya and tossed it back into the drawer. Sagely Lisle said, *You don't wear stuff like this. It's for some guy to see on you, and get turned on by it, and take it off you, and then he . . . you know — gets off on it. On you.*

Gets off on it. On you. Katya smiled at her sister's crude words, which were so succinct. Even if a guy loved you, or claimed he did, this was the transaction, essentially.

"You can make believe I'm a dead body lying here," Katya said suddenly, "like something in the morgue." These words came out without her knowing what she meant to say, nor what she meant by saying it; but she liked it that Marcus Kidder paused as he was repositioning a floor lamp with a blindingly strong bulb and said, frowning, "Katya, really! That's a morbid, childish thing to say. It's beauty that is our goal."

Beauty! Katya wanted to mutter *Bullshit* again but did not dare.

Strange to Katya now, posing for Marcus Kidder on the sexy black velvet cloth, in her sexy red silk lingerie that so resembled the lingerie her mother had hidden in her bureau drawer, that as minutes passed, she began to feel almost relaxed, hypnotized. *Like being a dead body on a slab in the morgue.* For Mr. Kidder behaved as if what he was doing was the most natural thing in the world. Katya smelled the pungent odor of acrylic paints, which was a sharp but pleasurable odor, and was soothed by the scratching sound of the artist's brush against the canvas. Only when Mr. Kidder abruptly laid down his brush and came to the sofa to smooth out the velvet cloth, or to reposition Katya's limbs, or to fan out Katya's hair across the back of the sofa behind her head, did Katya become tense, thinking, *Now he will touch me! He will lay his hands on me,* but in fact Mr. Kidder was matter-of-fact and professional, adjusting even Katya's head as if she were a mannequin. He did not even speak to her except to murmur, "Like this! Yes."

There was something peaceful about this. There was something mesmerizing about this. Though Katya still resented Marcus Kidder for coercing her into doing something she didn't want to do, yet how comforting it felt to give in. How comforting, to be able to please a man of such authority as Marcus Kidder — and how easy. *You only have to give in.*

"Mr. Kidder? Remember you said you had a mission for me? Is this it now, modeling, or is it something else?"

Clumsily Katya spoke, at the wrong time. Should've known that Mr. Kidder didn't want to be interrupted while he was painting her. He said, frowning, "It's premature to speak of that now, Katya. Right now we are embarked upon our quest for the perfect likeness. On a large canvas. Katya Spivak is too new in my life and too young for us to be speaking of such matters just now."

Katya was chastened. Katya was intrigued. Too young? Did this mean that Marcus Kidder expected to continue to see her beyond the summer? After she left Bayhead Harbor and returned to Vineland? She would return home on the day following Labor Day, and she would begin school at Vineland High the day following that. And Mr. Kidder was scheduled to return to New York City, as far as Katya knew from remarks he'd made.

There, Marcus Kidder lived on the fifteenth floor of an "old, antiquated, and very expensive" apartment building on Fifth Avenue, overlooking Central Park. He'd told Katya that she must come to visit him someday.

And how would I visit you, so far away in New York City? Katya was doubtful.

Juan will bring you, of course. Any time I bid him to do so. Any time Katya Spivak agrees.

Katya had laughed, uneasy. And yet excited, too. The wild thought came to her, *He wants to marry me! Or maybe to adopt me.*

Now Mr. Kidder was saying, in a gentle voice, "All in good time, Katya. This mission is not so easily accomplished. 'Happily ever after' is not so easily accomplished. For people like us, born at the wrong times."

Katya thought of her father suddenly. *Promise I'll be back, honey. For your birthday. Yes, Daddy will! Daddy promises.* Katya felt her throat constrict; she was in danger of crying. Wiping at her eyes, hoping that Mr. Kidder would not notice. (Of course Mr. Kidder noticed. Mr. Kidder noticed everything.) For the first time it occurred to Katya that her father, Jude Spivak, had not returned to Vineland as he'd promised because something had prevented him from returning, not because he'd forgotten his little daughter, or his family. Maybe he'd joined the army and gone away to fight in what newspapers called the Persian Gulf War, Operation Desert Storm, whatever that was, or had been. (Several of Katya's young male relatives had fought there. And older boys she'd known, graduates of Vineland High.) But sometime soon Jude Spivak might be able to return to Vineland, and Katya would see him again. *Katya, what has happened to you? Where is my daughter Katya? All growed up . . .*

The black velvet cloth was chafing Katya's skin. Suddenly she became restless, uneasy. "Mr. Kidder? How much longer? I — I don't feel well."

Annoyed, Mr. Kidder told her it would be a few minutes longer, please would she resume her position, stop squirming, and would she please lift her head, yes like that, "Eyes here, Katya," and would she smile, and Katya said weakly, "I — I want to leave, I guess. I don't want to be here," and Mr. Kidder said, frowning, "Katya, you know you will be paid. You must model professionally to be paid," and Katya said, sitting up, crossing her arms over her breasts, which were so shamefully exposed in the lacy top, and keeping her legs tightly crossed to hide the ugly little black spade tattoo, "I — I don't w-want money! I want to take off this fucking lingerie — I hate it! I hate this! I don't want your damned money, Mr. Kidder!" for suddenly it seemed to Katya that this was so. All along, this had been so!

"If you insist, Katya. But you are being very childish."

Mr. Kidder laid down his paintbrushes, unsmiling. Katya took little notice of him, hurried into the bathroom, where quickly she removed the red silk lingerie and changed back into her own familiar clothes: white cotton bra and cheap nylon undies, tank top just perceptibly discolored by sweat at the neckline, white shorts. She kicked her feet into her sandals. For some reason Katya's heart had begun to beat rapidly. She felt such fury for Marcus Kidder, seeing her shamefaced reflection in the mirror above the sink, that she could not bring herself to peer into her own eyes. *What a slut you are! Like your mother, Essie — look at you.* The hateful lingerie she'd have liked to tear into pieces but could not, so instead she wadded it into a ball and kicked it into a corner of the whitely gleaming, resplendent bathroom — hardly a bathroom but something like a powder room — where like a wounded creature it seemed to huddle. In a vase on a shelf was a bouquet of bizarrely colored fossil flowers, positioned to reflect in a floor-to-ceiling mirror with a dazzling effect. Katya saw her hand reach out, the hand of a bratty child, to snap the stem of an exquisite large crimson rose, which fell to the white tile floor, shattering.

"Katya? Is something wrong?"

Nervously Mr. Kidder knocked on the bathroom door. Katya had locked it behind her, and now she opened it, furious. In that instant Marcus Kidder must have seen the shattered crimson rose on the tile floor and the wadded red silk lingerie on the floor and, in Katya Spivak's face, a look of hysterical fury. "Let me go! Don't t-try to stop me! I — I shouldn't be here! I'm going now." Rudely Katya pushed past the startled man, her lips moving in a furious mutter: *Dirty old man, what right d'you have, like the Engelhardts what right, damn you, hate you.* Katya snatched up her straw handbag and headed for the door. In distress, Marcus Kidder followed after her, apologizing: "Dear Katya! What on earth has happened? This was just a — an experiment, in vivid colors and in silk. Silken cloth and silken skin. Like Renoir —" Katya was thinking, *I can walk out of here, I won't come back. I don't need this man's money,* yet — so strangely! — as if this were a dream in which she were trying to make her way through a dense, clutching substance like muck, she paused at the door, paused panting and trembling at the open door, feeling again that choking sensation in her throat, which made her want to cry; and perhaps Katya was crying, for how could she behave like this to Marcus Kidder, who was so kind to her, and such a gentleman — so much nicer to Katya than her own grandfather had ever been, and seeing in her such promise, such worth and such specialness, which no one in Vineland had ever seen in Katya Spivak, including even her father. Katya stood in the doorway at the rear of Mr. Kidder's studio and could not seem to step out onto the terrace and run away. Panting like a dog that has been trained by his master and can't break out of his training, though his training has hurt, humbled, humiliated him and enslaved him.

And so Katya stood in the doorway of Mr. Kidder's studio looking out toward the Atlantic Ocean, where agitated white-capped waves were just visible in the waning sunlight, and quietly Mr. Kidder came up behind her, knowing not to speak at first, for speaking to Katya would only arouse her further. Gently, Mr. Kidder stroked her hair, as you might stroke the fur of a frightened animal; Mr. Kidder stroked her shoulder, and her arm; Mr. Kidder circled her wrist with his long, elegantly shaped fingers, but very lightly. For Marcus Kidder was always gentle with Katya, in his formal, gentlemanly way. And Marcus Kidder would not fail to pay her, she knew.

"Katya, I will never make such a request of you again. I've hurt you, I can see."

Mr. Kidder turned Katya, gripping her shoulders, gently gripping her shoulders and holding her firmly. And her eyes lifted to his and she saw that he was genuinely repentant. And had he hurt her, really? Not really. The red silk lingerie was a joke, nothing more. Katya Spivak was tough, and Katya Spivak was smart. Like all the Spivaks, Katya was expecting to be paid.

Mr. Kidder took Katya's hand and unclenched her fingers so that he could press into her hand a wad of neatly folded bills. "You know that I adore you, Katya. I seek only your perfect likeness — to ennoble you. Have faith in me! You will see."

Katya's stiff fingers closed about the bills, as always Katya's fingers did. Good! There was this payment, at least.

"And I think that you have some feeling for me, Katya? Am I mistaken?"

Marcus Kidder's backward way of speaking! Katya stood silent, gnawing at her lower lip. The choking sensation returned in her throat. She could hardly bear to look at Marcus Kidder's handsome ruined face, those eyes that were so beautiful to her, so filled with love for her, pouched in darkish crinkled flesh.

"Forgive me, Katya! Next time will be very different, I promise."

Katya stiffened against Mr. Kidder's embrace but did not resist. And his lips against the side of her head, his warm breath in her hair, against her cheek; slowly, hesitantly, moving against her mouth.

And then suddenly Mr. Kidder was kissing Katya. And Katya, dazed, scarcely knowing what she did, stood still and childlike as if in obedience, in his arms, and, in the surprise of the moment, responded to his kiss, as she might have responded to the kiss of any man, or boy, for whom she felt a strong emotion; for Mr. Kidder's lips were so warm, so soft and comforting, and made no demands upon her, and Katya was so lonely suddenly, and close to tears.

She pushed herself away. She ran along the flagstone path, clutching her straw bag, clutching the bills in her clenched fist, before Mr. Kidder could follow after her and say goodbye to her at the front gate.

Blocks away Katya opened her fist, paused to count the bills in the reflected light of a drugstore window: five twenty-dollar bills. Five! Crisp and stiff as if freshly minted.

19

No kiss is forgotten; it resides in the memory as in the flesh, and so Katya many times felt the press of Marcus Kidder's warm mouth on hers in the days and especially in the nights following. And her heartbeat quickened in protest: *How could you! Kiss him! That old man! Kiss him! Let him put his arms around you and kiss you and kiss him back! The old man's mouth and Katya Spivak's mouth! How could you.*

The five twenty-dollar bills Katya hid away carefully with the other bills her friend had given her: two hundred and sixty dollars.

20

"Who's it? Oh, Katya! Honey, hel*lo*."

Finally Katya's mother answered the phone. How many times Katya had dialed her number. At last Essie Spivak answered the phone.

At first she sounded hostile. And groggy, as if Katya's call had wakened her from sleep. But she didn't sound drunk, or seriously angry. In fact, Essie was sounding cheery now, as if happy to hear from Katya, as if someone was nudging her, saying, *This is your daughter! Your daughter who did you a favor! C'mon, Essie, be nice.* Though Essie hadn't taken time to call Katya, she seemed genuinely pleased to have a call *from* Katya, though in the middle of the day (at 3:30 P.M.? was this possible?) she did sound as if she was just waking up. Katya saw her mother dazedly smiling and running quick fingers through her spiky dyed-beet hair as she asked Katya, how was she? How were the Eggensteins treating her? How many more weeks before Katya would be back home? Only then remembering the check that Katya had sent several weeks before and thanking her profusely for it: "That was sweet of you, Katya! My sweet girl. I'd about given up hope, and there's my best girl, my sweet Katya, coming to her mom's rescue. Your snotty sisters — know what? Wouldn't even answer my calls."

Uneasily Katya waited for her mother to become suspicious and ask who Marcus C. Kidder was, who'd made out the check, but to her surprise, her mother took up another topic, how her luck had changed in Atlantic City, where she'd won big at the Taj, where she'd always had good luck, or mostly good luck. She'd met this "sweet, really decent guy," an "actual doctor" — "gasto-intesticular specialist" — from Morristown, who'd staked her at blackjack and helped with the down payment on her new 1989 Mercury Grand Marquis . . . Katya pressed the phone tight against her ear as her mother's excited voice wavered in and out of earshot; there was static, and Essie's voice was raised. "Katya? You still there? Know who wants to drive up there and see you? Roy Mraz — your crazy cousin Roy? He's through rehab and more grown-up, kind of a sweet kid, or can be . . . Want me to give him your number there, Katya?" And quickly Katya said no, the Engelhardts didn't want her to take personal calls, especially from guys; and so Katya's mother said, "You could reach him at Fritzie's garage, I guess. Call him."

After Katya hung up she felt dazed, disoriented, realizing that she'd forgotten to ask her mother about repaying the three hundred dollars, for hadn't it been a loan?

Had it been a loan, from Mr. Kidder? Or a gift?

21

I will not.

Wasn't going to call Roy Mraz, and wasn't going to see Marcus Kidder again.

In Harbor Park she took out her sketchpad and colored pencils. While Tricia squealed with the other children flinging bits of bread at the excited waterfowl, Katya sat on a bench with baby Kevin in his stroller beside her and sketched the scene: swans, Canada geese, white geese, and mallard ducks in a swarm of squawking and wing-flapping, all of them beautiful birds and yet comical in their behavior. More comical were the actions of sparrows flying into the melee to dart beneath the larger birds and make off with pieces of bread beneath their very beaks. You had to laugh aloud to see tiny birds flying away with chunks of bread in their beaks nearly as large as their heads . . . Katya's fingers didn't move so swiftly or so deftly as Marcus Kidder's fingers when sketching her in his studio, but her drawings weren't bad, Katya thought. The trick was, as Mr. Kidder instructed, to *see* before you began to sketch; if you tried to sketch too quickly, without *seeing*, you would mess up. In grade school Katya had been praised by her teachers for her crayon drawings that told little stories, like comic strips, but her sister Tracey disillusioned her by saying that grade school teachers praised anyone who wasn't retarded, practically, and that Katya shouldn't take such praise seriously. But now, since *Funny Bunny* and the other children's books Katya had been reading aloud to Tricia, she'd begun to think, *I could do books like these myself. Maybe!*

In Vineland, in the houses of women for whom Katya frequently babysat, there had been no children's books for Katya to read from, to the children; the TV was always on, whether anyone watched it or not. In Bayhead Harbor, in households like the Engelhardts', all the children were given books, beautifully illustrated storybooks featuring animals like Funny Bunny who could talk and think like people and made you smile. Sometimes the books were scary, but never too scary; always they ended happily. What was surprising to Katya was how expensive the books were. Only people with money would buy them, and though you could take such books out of the public library, only people with money seemed to know or to care about this. In the Vineland households Katya Spivak knew, there were no books, and few newspapers: just TV.

Katya shivered, thinking of this. She didn't want to return to Vineland! She'd begun to be frightened of Vineland.

"Excuse me. You are Katya?"

Out of nowhere he appeared. A soft-spoken man in his late thirties perhaps, in dark jacket, dark slacks, and white shirt open at the throat, wearing a visored cap like a chauffeur and dark glasses. "I am driver for Mr. Kidder. Here is something I am to give you."

Taken by surprise, Katya could only accept what the man handed her: an oversized envelope made of red construction paper, addressed in tall block letters TO KATYA.

Katya opened the envelope, removed a folded sheet of stiff construction paper, and read:

Dearest Katya,
    I am sorry. Forgive and come today to tea-time on the terrace and bring the children with you. The promise is all fun and no regrets and a short ride with Juan at the wheel.

                Mopey-blue with missing you,
                   your friend
                    Marcus Kidder

Mopey-blue. Katya smiled to think of Marcus Kidder as mopey and blue on her account, but quickly she folded up the letter and told Juan the driver, "Tell him — Mr. Kidder — that I can't. Thank him for me but — I can't."

Gravely the driver said, "Then there is this I am to give you."

A second envelope? This made of sky-blue construction paper addressed in tall block letters TO KATYA.

Dearest Katya,
    I understand! In fact, I predicted! On such short notice you can't bring the children of course.
    And so will you come at another time, alone? Tomorrow after dusk? Shall I hope?
    Promise only just fun and no regrets and a very beautiful very special gift awaits my very beautiful very special Katya, you will see!

                                        Mopey-blue with missing you,
                                        your friend
                                        Marcus Kidder

Katya laughed nervously. Feeling her face heating. *Very special very beautiful:* Marcus Kidder had such a way of writing, you could hear Funny Bunny in his voice. Katya felt the temptation to give in but again told the driver, "No, thank you — tell Mr. Kidder that I can't. I'm s-sorry." Katya faltered as if her throat were shutting up. "I can't."

In a gravely formal voice, the dark-uniformed driver thanked Katya and turned away. Katya sprang to her feet and watched him cross a grassy stretch of parkland to the parking lot, where a long, gleaming black Lincoln Town Car with tinted windows was parked conspicuously. Mr. Kidder's limousine! Katya stared in amazement. Mr. Kidder had sent that limousine for *her.*

By this time the other nannies were watching her curiously. How strange it was to Katya Spivak, to be so publicly singled out, made to feel privileged, yet uneasy. And now she realized she'd seen that hearselike sedan just recently, on New Liberty Street near the Engelhardts' house, and while walking to the public beach on East Pond Road, which was an unpaved road, with no sidewalk, so that you walked at the side of the road. At the time Katya had taken little notice of the elegant black car that seemed to be following at a little distance behind her; she'd assumed it was a coincidence, not related to her at all. Now she had to wonder if the driver, Juan, had been sent to spy on her, or if Mr. Kidder himself had been inside, in the back seat, behind tinted windows, spying on her.

Maybe Mr. Kidder had expected Katya to see him? A Funny Bunny kind of thing to do, like playing hide-and-seek.

He wouldn't want to scare me. Not me.

This was so, Katya knew. Marcus Kidder would never want to scare *her*.

And yet there was a word for this sort of thing: *stalking*.

At least two of Katya's mother's man friends had stalked her after they'd broken up. Showing up outside the clinic where Essie had worked at the time, offering her a ride home. In stores, at the mall, on the street, meeting her "by accident." The most persistent of the stalkers had been Artie, who'd called Essie so many times she'd had to have her telephone number changed, and one scary time that Katya was remembering now he'd showed up in his car outside Katya's school to ask if she'd like a ride home . . . *Can't shake the bastards off*, Essie said. *They have to be the ones to lose interest, not you.*

Eventually Artie had given up, or disappeared. In Vineland, men often disappeared. A certain type of man disappeared.

But Marcus Kidder was not that type of man.

"Kat-cha? Is somethin' wrong?"

There stood Tricia Engelhardt, worriedly sucking at a finger. Tricia had used up all the bread Katya had given her, and still the clamorous waterfowl were hungry. Katya assured the little girl that she was fine, of course nothing was wrong, but it was time for them to get back home.

Really it wasn't time. They hadn't been in the park nearly as long as they usually were. But Katya clutched the little girl by the hand, pushed baby Kevin in his stroller, in the corner of her eye seeing the sleek, gleaming black Lincoln Town Car pull out of the parking lot and depart, silent and smooth-gliding as an undersea predator.

Go away! Go away! I don't love you! I hate it that you love me.

22

HERE WAS PROOF she could stay away.

From Marcus Kidder, she could stay away.

His offers of presents for her, payment for "modeling" — she could refuse.

And his kisses. And his love. She could refuse.

"You can come with us Sunday afternoon, to Cape May? On your half-day off?" Mrs. Engelhardt spoke with faint incredulity, as if she hadn't heard Katya clearly.

Katya said yes, if Mrs. Engelhardt could use her. If there was room for her on the yacht. Katya spoke humbly, as one requesting a special favor, even though she understood — and her employer understood — that her presence on the yacht trip with visiting friends of the Engelhardts who'd brought along two small children would be invaluable.

Yet canny Lorraine Engelhardt didn't say, *Katya! You're a lifesaver* but, with a measured smile, "We can't pay you for overtime, though. Just regular time. If you understand that."

Eagerly Katya nodded. She understood!

And so Katya accompanied the Engelhardts and their friends on a windblown excursion south along the Jersey coast to Cape May, where they visited relatives; and Katya was enormously helpful, taking care of the restless children and the adults both, serving drinks, mopping up spills, in every way the sweet-smiling hired girl who knew her place; and the Engelhardts were grateful for her presence and seemed to like her again, as they'd seemed to like her before Marcus Kidder. For Katya wanted to be liked, there was this weakness in her: desperately she wanted to be liked, even by people she resented. For these were rich people, the Engelhardts and their flashy friends, and you never knew, as Essie Spivak said, when a person with money might spend some on you.

Katya's mother meant men. That was the attraction of Atlantic City. A taste for gambling meant gambling of all kinds.

But no. It was foolish of Katya to imagine that the Engelhardts from Saddle River would do anything for her. What a futile wish!

Katya knew that she was expendable to these people. They were consumers, users — they used people up and discarded them. No matter if Tricia adored her nanny; Katya Spivak was just a girl hired for the summer who wouldn't be rehired next year. For Mrs. Engelhardt had hired Katya only because other girls had turned her down, girls who'd wanted to be paid more than the minimum wage.

Girls who knew that Lorraine Engelhardt was a mean-spirited woman, and cheap. (The sheets on the nanny's bed and the towels in the nanny's lavatory were frayed and thin from numerous launderings. Even the light-bulb wattage in the nanny's quarters was low.) And Max Engelhardt after a few drinks had a way of looking at you with a slovenly, damp smile, his eyes crawling over you like ants. *Could give you a good time, baby. You know that, eh!*

Max Engelhardt steering the noisy Chris-Craft bouncing and bucking through the choppy waves off the Jersey shore, and Katya had to take him his drink in a plastic cup and stand beside him listening to him talk boastfully as a chilly wind whipped at her hair and made her eyes water, and in her loneliness Katya was thinking of Marcus Kidder prying open her fingers, pressing bills into her hand (for he would always pay her, he had promised); Marcus Kidder saying he adored her and would "ennoble" her; painting her portrait, which would be seen and admired by strangers; kissing Katya's mouth so warmly, gently, as Katya had never been kissed before, and how strange and wonderful it was, how she'd begun kissing Marcus Kidder in return, and had lifted her arms to embrace him.

On the floor of the yacht at her feet Katya later discovered a pair of dice that had fallen out of a board game called Casino. Katya shook the dice in her hand, thinking, *If it comes up six or more, I will see Mr. Kidder again. If not, I will not.*

Tossing the dice, and up came nine.

23

"WHY, KATYA! You've come."

It had been arranged: Mr. Kidder's driver would pick Katya up a half-block from the Engelhardts' house, to take her in the long black Lincoln Town Car to the rear of the beautiful old shingle-board house at 17 Proxmire Street. And at the rear of the house, beneath a shadowy wisteria arbor, there stood Marcus Kidder, leaning on his cane, awaiting her.

It was late, past 11 P.M. Finally the Engelhardts' house had darkened; and at 17 Proxmire, Mr. Kidder's house, seen from the street, appeared to be darkened.

Nervously Katya greeted her elderly friend. Her elderly lover, she had to think of him. Though in the half-light, smiling so warmly at her, and so very tall and straight-backed, Mr. Kidder could have been mistaken for a much younger man.

They greeted each other by clasping hands. Mr. Kidder brushed his lips against Katya's cheek and embraced her, causing Katya to stagger off-balance, nervously laughing, resisting the instinct to lift her elbows against him. She smelled a familiar sweetly sour odor on his breath. *He's been drinking*, Katya thought. *He's afraid of me.*

"Dear girl! I am so happy to see you . . ." Mr. Kidder began kissing Katya's hands in an exaggerated way, making wet smacking noises as you might with a child, to make the child shiver and laugh. For always Marcus Kidder had to exert control by such clownish behavior. Katya hoped that his driver, Juan, parking the limousine inside the garage, hadn't noticed.

His arm around Katya's shoulders, Mr. Kidder led Katya into

the house. Through a dark maze of a garden where rose thorns pricked her, to the flagstone terrace at the rear of the house, where only a solitary outdoor light was burning, and into Mr. Kidder's studio, with its comforting smell of paints. Katya was startled to feel how familiar this room had come to seem to her, a kind of refuge, a secret place which no one except Mr. Kidder and Katya Spivak knew of. It did not cross her mind to wonder if the other girls and women whose portraits were hanging in shadow, on the wall, had come to feel the same way, in their separate times.

"Welcome back! I haven't been able to paint — I've hardly been able to sleep — since . . . last week." Another time Marcus Kidder brushed his warm, dry lips against the side of Katya's face, in a restrained and unthreatening manner. The thought came to Katya, *This man loves me! In this room it happened.*

There was magic in this revelation. Katya felt her throat constrict with the need to cry.

Mr. Kidder hadn't turned on the bright studio lights but only smaller lights, from table lamps. Above the fireplace mantel was a mirror reflecting the young blond girl and the older white-haired man as if through a scrim, with no sharp edges. On the mantel a jewel-like old-fashioned clock that Katya hadn't seen before was ticking with comforting authority, flanked by vases of fossil flowers, which gleamed and glittered like winking eyes. And in the background, a fluid dreamlike music of exquisite beauty, like water rippling gently over stones.

Briskly Mr. Kidder rubbed his hands together. In a deadpan voice, he informed Katya that "ever-busy Mrs. Bee" had gone away for several days, leaving him quite alone: "Unless Mrs. Bee is horribly trapped in an attic room of this vast old house, buzzing and hurtling herself against an unyielding pane of glass."

This was funny! Katya had to laugh at the spectacle of Mrs. Bee reduced to bee size, buzzing and hurtling herself against an attic window.

"A drink, Katya? Must have a drink, to celebrate the prodigal model's return."

As if Katya had stayed away a very long time, instead of less than a week.

It had been five days. To one who loves, a lifetime.

It was clear: Mr. Kidder seemed edgier, more excited than usual. His fingers trembled just slightly as he poured wine into two long-stemmed glasses: a nearly full glass for himself, and for Katya a precisely measured one third dark red wine mixed with two thirds sparkling water from a tall green bottle with a French label.

"I can drink wine straight, Mr. Kidder," Katya objected. "I'm not ten years old."

"Indeed you are not, dear Katya. You'd quite prepared me, when first we met, by declaring that you had 'bad habits' — of which in the intervening weeks we have seen little, to my disappointment. Yet for all your charming 'bad habits,' you remain but a minor in the vigilant state of New Jersey."

Nonetheless, Mr. Kidder raised his glass in a toast — "To the 'perfect likeness,' and to her pursuer" — clicked his glass against Katya's glass, and drank. And Katya drank.

What a dark, feral taste this wine had, a surprise to Katya, who'd expected something like the sugary-sweet local wine she'd been given at parties. Even diluted with sparkling water, this drink made her mouth pucker.

Gently Mr. Kidder chided, "Wine is to be sipped, Katya. Not drunk. If you're thirsty, dear, now or while you're posing for your portrait, please drink sparkling water."

So there was to be another modeling session, that night. Katya had assumed this would be so. But not in the ridiculous red silk lingerie tonight!

Since she'd seen him waiting for her beneath the wisteria arbor, like a gentleman lover in an old storybook illustration, Katya had felt a thrill of warmth for Marcus Kidder; such strong affection, maybe she did love him. Yet her Spivak soul stood detached, calculating, *If he paid me one hundred dollars last time, he will pay me more this time . . .*

He'd have found the torn, mangled, wadded red silk lingerie on the floor of the bathroom where Katya had kicked it. He'd have known how Katya had hated posing in such a costume, how she'd abased herself only for him.

"Mr. Kidder —"

"Marcus, please call me. Mr. Kidder is — was — my elderly father, a businessman of such limited imagination and verve, he scarcely deserves *you.*"

"M-Marcus." Katya spoke uncertainly, feeling suddenly shy.

"Mar-cus. Best pronounced as a spondee, dear."

Katya had no idea what a spondee was. *Mar-cus:* equal stress on both syllables.

"The music you are hearing, Katya — it's the music of Ravel, transcribed for harp. Do you like it?"

"It's beautiful, Mr. Kidder." Politely Katya spoke, and then amended: "Mar-cus."

"It is indeed beautiful. It is specially chosen for tonight. You might study harp, you know, Katya — and let your hair grow long, glimmering and wavy down your back."

There was a strange excitement between them. A kind of electrical tension, as in the air before a storm. Katya wondered if Mr. Kidder had not expected her to return to him, and if this might be turned to her advantage.

"Will you sit down, Katya? I assume that you've been working much of this day, for Mrs. Mayfly and the children. And what a good little nanny you've been, like Cinderella — who never complained either, though her wicked employer made her sleep in the ashes."

Katya sat, on the sofa. Mr. Kidder sat close beside her, but not unnervingly close. You could see that he was trying not to upset his young-girl visitor; he was determined to remain a gentleman, that she might come to him. Katya had many times imagined that as soon as they were alone together, Mr. Kidder would kiss her, as he'd kissed her five days ago; yet he'd only just brushed his lips against her face, and now just touched the back of her hand as he spoke, and lightly stroked her wrist. His breathing was quickened, urgent. Katya could see that he'd prepared for this evening: his long, lean, clean-shaven jaws seemed to glow, and gave off a sharp wintergreen scent; his very white hair was neatly combed, and seemed to spring back from his forehead with vigor. How bright, alert, and intelligent the vivid blue eyes, and how warmly flushed his skin! In the lamplight Katya could barely discern the network of lines in his face, furrows in his high forehead and strange vertical lines in his cheeks, like rivulets of tears, which imparted an air of sculpted dignity. Mr. Kidder was wearing summer trousers with a sharp crease and a cream-colored dress shirt left unbuttoned at the throat to display a swirl of glinting hairs. In an impassioned voice he was saying, "I've been concerned that I might have lost you, Katya. That I'd said — and done — unforgivable things, and you would not want to see me again. After I'd declared myself so frankly to you — when your lovely portrait is at last emerging out of the chaos of empty canvas . . ."

Katya felt the impulse to laugh wildly. Such extravagant things Marcus Kidder said to her! Yet she was deeply moved, too, and wanted to assure Mr. Kidder that yes, she'd returned to him, and would model for him again.

Katya sipped her drink. The wine taste seemed to be improving. A fizzing sensation rose into her nostrils, making her want to sneeze.

"This feeling between us, Katya, which sprang into life that morning on Ocean Avenue, and which I'm trying to capture in art — you do feel it, dear, don't you? That we are soul mates, born at awkward times?"

Katya bit her lower lip, murmuring what sounded like "I guess."

"You do mean it, Katya? You're not just saying this to humor me?"

Humor? Katya wasn't sure what this meant. Unless Mr. Kidder was asking if she was lying to placate him. As girls and women do, to placate men.

"Though surely I can love enough for both of us, dear. If you will let me."

They sat stricken in silence. Mr. Kidder was stroking the back of Katya's hand, but he did not otherwise touch her. If he had, if he'd embraced her, Katya was thinking weakly that she could not pull away from him; she would lay her head against his shoulder, press her face against his neck . . . She could not resist Marcus Kidder in this moment, for there was no one in all of the world who so valued Katya Spivak as Marcus Kidder did. She thought, *He would forgive me anything, he loves me so.*

Impulsively then Katya said, "You never told me who Naomi was, Mr. Kidder." In her flat Jersey voice quickly amending, "Mar-cus."

"Naomi was a very sweet girl of long ago, dear. A lesser Katya — an unrealized and incomplete Katya."

"Was she related to you? Was she . . . your daughter?"

"No. She was not."

Though Mr. Kidder had stiffened in displeasure and had ceased stroking Katya's hand, Katya persisted. "Who was she, then? Did you love her?"

"I advise you to forget about Naomi, dear. There are some very minor riddles never to be solved."

"But this Naomi was born closer to the time you were born, Mr. Kidder, than I was, wasn't she? 'Nineteen thirty-nine to nineteen fifty-six.'"

Mr. Kidder stared at Katya, astonished. "But — how do you know that?"

"I saw the book. The book in the library you'd dedicated to her. The picture book about the little skunk's first day at school, which I've been reading to Tricia Engelhardt. It's a wonderful story, Mr. Kidder. I saw the dedication — 'To my lost Naomi.'"

Now Mr. Kidder drew back from Katya. His smile faded.

"'To my lost Naomi' — I'd forgotten."

"Was Naomi your soul mate, too? How could you forget your soul mate?"

The dark, feral wine beat through Katya's veins, urging her to utter such words. For in that moment Katya was meanly jealous of the other girl, the rich blond girl with the sweet vacant gaze.

A shrill sort of sex banter, this was. Katya could hear the crudeness of her south Jersey speech, yet could not seem to overcome it.

Carefully Mr. Kidder was saying, "Naomi belongs to my private life, Katya. My life before you. She was in fact the daughter of Bayhead Harbor friends, and she died young of a wasting disease similar to but not identical with multiple sclerosis. She resides in my memory, but she does not live now as you do, dear Katya. So please drop the subject."

Still Katya persisted. Her mouth twisted in bitterness, which was also a kind of mockery she'd seen in Essie Spivak.

"And what about the other girls? The women? That woman with the red, wavy hair" — Katya was pointing at one of the portraits, prominent on the wall — "who was she?"

"Enough, Katya! It is always risky when a model chooses to speak."

Mr. Kidder was on his feet. Brisk now, and matter-of-fact. Perhaps he was amused by his young friend's childishness. Perhaps he was dismayed, disgusted. He gave no sign but began to work, switching on brighter lights, bringing over his easel to set in front of the sofa. Katya was feeling remorseful now. Draining her glass and coughing. How crude she was! She knew this. How stupid, to reveal her jealousy. It was a mistake to provoke Marcus Kidder. She'd come to his studio to pose for him, after all, and to be paid.

[122]

She'd dressed with more than usual care, and she'd even put on lipstick. *Slut. Slut! Pay me.*

"Come, Katya. We haven't much time."

Nearly midnight! Katya felt a swoon of anxiety and remorse.

Briskly Mr. Kidder adjusted the sofa, took away the small pillows, smoothed out the black velvet backdrop. From a nearby table he took up a small white blanket, or shawl, which Katya had been noticing: was this the very beautiful, very special present he'd promised her if she returned to him? It did look beautiful, crocheted and decorated with small white satin ribbons. Casually Mr. Kidder said, "Tonight, Katya, you will remove your clothes."

Katya wasn't sure she'd heard correctly. Remove her clothes?

"Your clothes, Katya. You can't seriously think that I would paint you in your summer play-clothes, do you? You can take off your clothes in the bathroom and wrap yourself in this shawl, which is for you. Cashmere and silk, hand-crocheted, from Portugal. For you."

Seeing how Katya continued to stare at him, so taken by surprise that she wasn't yet upset, Mr. Kidder said patiently, "Don't be a child, Katya. A model models – the human body is the subject, and in serious art the human body is usually nude. Nude, not naked. There is a distinction."

Slowly Katya shook her head. *No.*

"Katya, *yes.* Go into the other room, remove your silly sport clothes, wrap yourself in this lovely shawl, and come out here like a professional model. You know that I will pay you, dear? Yes?"

Mr. Kidder was holding out to Katya the white cashmere-and-silk shawl, quite a large shawl, with a delicate fringe, feathery light. It was true, the shawl was beautiful. Casually it might be revealed to Lorraine Engelhardt, drawn over Katya's shoulders on the next windy boat ride on the ocean.

"I d-don't think so, Mr. Kidder. I guess — I don't want to pose . . . nude." Almost Katya choked on the very word: *nude.*

Mr. Kidder objected: "Katya, your wants are irrelevant here. We are seeking something beyond mere wants — moods. Think of your soul revealed by way of your body, and the artist is the instrument to make it luminous, as art."

Yet Katya said, numbly, "I — I don't know what that means, Mr. Kidder. But I don't want to do it. I'm not really a . . . model. I'm not even very pretty. I don't have any talent for art." Words tumbled from Katya's mouth; she had scarcely any idea what she was saying. "The sketchpad you gave me, the pencils — I tried to use them, in Harbor Park, drawing geese, but — "

"Katya, stop! You're being ridiculous. I will not allow you to denigrate yourself — your beauty, and your talent. I'm sure that if you work hard and use your imagination, you can one day write and illustrate children's books just as well as Marcus Cullen Kidder did in his time. How will you know, until you try? All that lies ahead, dear. Within the scope of my wishes for you. But that is the future, and tonight is now. You will disrobe in the bathroom and wrap yourself in this shawl. Now."

Katya took the shawl from Mr. Kidder. Light as gossamer in her hands, the most beautiful shawl she had ever held.

Yet still, with childlike stubbornness, Katya shook her head. No. She could not do this. She wasn't beautiful, as Mr. Kidder said, but ordinary, ugly. Anyone who saw her naked — nude — would laugh at her.

Exasperated, Mr. Kidder drew down from a bookshelf a hefty book titled *The Female Nude,* to show Katya. Here were glossy color plates of female nudes by such artists as Titian, Botticelli, Giorgione, Raphael, Ingres, Rubens, Renoir, Manet, Matisse . . . Katya stared at the color plates with mounting impatience as Mr. Kidder paged through them, pausing to speak of them. You could see that Marcus Kidder was not a man to be contradicted; his gentlemanly good nature was possible only when he was obeyed in all things. When he encountered opposition, he became infuriated. And this was so, Katya thought, for all the men she'd known, including her father. *You do not contradict a man. If you want him to love you, you do not.*

Katya saw that as Mr. Kidder loomed above her, oily moisture gleamed on his high, bony forehead, and he was pressing the heel of his hand against his chest, where you'd expect his heart to be. The expression on his face was both stricken and indignant, as if pain itself were an insult to him. In dismay, Katya thought, *Mr. Kidder is not a well man! That is his secret.*

"We're wasting time. For me, a man of my age, precious time. Disrobe, Katya, and wrap yourself in this shawl. Come back out here, and if lying on the sofa you don't feel that you can remove the shawl, or allow me to remove it, that will be all right. It won't be ideal, but I can proceed." Mr. Kidder took up Katya's wineglass, replenished it with a half-glass of wine and a half-glass of sparkling water, and handed it to her, and poured himself another full glass and drank. He was not so agitated now; the pressure in his chest must have faded.

Katya thought, *He wants to get me drunk. That's a good idea.* She drank; she hiccupped and laughed and wiped her mouth on the edge of her hand. She said, "You must know what a naked — nude — female looks like, Mr. Kidder. Why d'you need me?" and Mr. Kidder said, "Because you are you, Katya," and Katya said, "My body could be any girl's body, Mr. Kidder. It's just something I was born into," and Mr. Kidder said, "Well, yes — as I was born into the body of Marcus Cullen Kidder. This is so. You are quite the Platonist, Katya! Yet Plato would argue that your body is but a vessel for your soul: your perfect body is the vessel for your perfect soul. And it is your soul, Katya, that I wish to portray. You come to me at a crucial hour of my life, as it is a late hour of my life — you are my soul mate, and I will never give you up."

Katya was moved by this speech, and made uneasy by it. She drank from the wineglass, not sipping but frankly drinking as if thirsty. The dark, feral wine taste seemed delicious to her now. Like Roy Mraz's open-mouthed kisses, sucking and gnawing kisses, like Roy Mraz's rough hands on her body — you wanted to scream for Roy to stop what he was doing and then you screamed because Roy might be about to stop. Helplessly she thought, *I won't do this — I will walk out of here.* More reasonably she thought, *He will pay me more than he has paid me yet. He loves me.*

As if something had been decided, and in his favor, Marcus Kidder began whistling. Shoved his arms into a paint-splattered smock to wear over his gentleman's clothes, and prepared his brushes. Chiding Katya, he said, "We must use the ever-diminishing time that remains to us, Katya! Time is the enemy of lovers. Worse even than the frank light of day."

Katya laughed and set down her emptied wineglass, clumsily, so that it toppled over onto the floor. On unsteady legs she went into the whitely gleaming bathroom to remove her clothes. The beautiful white cashmere-and-silk shawl she took with her, to wrap about her nude body.

He is the only one who loves me. And I love him.
  He's a dirty old man, a pervert. You must know.
  Marcus Kidder! Not ever.
  A gentleman-pervert. A rich-old-man pervert.
  He adores me. He adores Katya, he believes in her.
  There is no Katya — it's all in his head! What a joke.
  He gave me money for Momma when no one else would. He pays me, and he loves me. And I love him.
  For his money, bitch. We know.

When Katya reappeared, moving awkwardly — drunkenly? — in the shawl wrapped about her, which fortunately was the size of a child's blanket, Mr. Kidder behind his easel no more than glanced at her with seeming casualness. He instructed her to lie down on the sofa, as she'd done before, and this time to lift and cross her arms behind her head — "In the most natural pose you can manage. And relax." He seemed not to care whether Katya fastidiously covered herself with the shawl or not. Stiffly she tried to obey him while keeping the shawl over her breasts and keeping her knees pressed tightly together; she had a horror of the sharp-eyed artist seeing the ugly little black spade tattoo on her inner thigh and guessing at once what it was.

The claim of another. A crude sex-claim.

Or had it been one of Roy Mraz's jokes? He'd been high, and Katya had been so dazed she'd barely remembered afterward the stinging pain of the tattoo artist's needle . . .

"Katya, eyes here! Please don't lapse into your mysterious melancholy. We are here, it is now. All else *verboten*." After this, Mr. Kidder fell silent. Katya could hear just the comforting sound of his brush against the canvas and in the background the rippling harp music. In a kind of floating dream she was aware of the cozily lit studio, Mr. Kidder's beautiful, tasteful things: wicker furniture, hardwood floor, elegant venetian blinds shut tight against lattice windows, the tick of the mantel clock. Glittering clusters of fossil flowers, so lifelike you might mistake them for living flowers encased in glass, their beauty suffocated and preserved.

And, from outside, the *slap-slap-slap* of the surf.

The dark-tasting wine had made Katya sleepy. Her thoughts came slow and silent and remote as high cumulus clouds. By degrees the white shawl slipped open, exposing her hard, rounded, creamy-pale little breasts with their nipples like mashed strawberries . . . In the bathroom earlier Katya had removed her clothes with fumbling fingers, avoiding her reflection in the mirror, her flushed face, her shamed eyes; quickly she'd wrapped herself in the shawl to hide her nakedness. For there is no fear more primitive than the fear of being naked in a strange place. But now, so relaxed, her eyelids drooping, Katya was thinking that Mr. Kidder was right, as usual: the human body was a subject for art. In

The Female Nude there were dazzling works of art, centuries-old paintings of surpassing beauty; the female nude was a revered subject for the greatest artists, and Marcus Kidder was of this lineage. For this was true art and nothing like the lewd, lurid billboards looming above the Garden State Parkway featuring exotic dancers at the Atlantic City casinos . . .

No shame to it, if you are paid. Models are paid.

The higher the payment, the less shame.

What time was it? Katya tried to make out the clock face, which was obscured by shadow. Tried to see through her eyelids, which appeared to be shut, her eyelids so heavy she could not lift them. And her arms, and her legs, leaden, impossible to move. Her knees had fallen open; the black spade tattoo must have been exposed. The shawl had slipped from her entirely, or had been drawn away by invisible hands. The black velvet cloth crinkled beneath her, chafed the sensitive skin of her back and buttocks. Her breath had grown husky and labored, as if she were sleeping, though — Katya was sure! — she was not sleeping but alert and awake. And now someone was leaning over her, and a man's lips lightly touched hers. And she felt a yearning to be kissed, to be held and to be kissed, to be loved, protected. For there is no fear so primitive as the fear of being not-loved, and not-protected. The *slap-slap-slap* of the waves was hypnotic, and yet: the fact of the ocean is that it is harsh and inhuman, and wading out into the surf, you can be overcome by an abrupt crashing wave, picked up, thrown down, your mouth filled with salty water and sand; within seconds you can drown if you are not-loved, and not-protected. *My darling! My beautiful girl!* — as she lay unable to move, unable to open her eyes, sinking further into darkness which was both suffocating and comforting. She felt her nipples lose their childish softness and become taut like hard little berries, sensitive when touched. A man's wet lips were on her breasts, he was sucking her breasts; Katya could not see his face, she squirmed in protest, tried to speak but could not speak, she was laughing because it tickled so, there was a sudden sensation in her belly, between her legs, a kind of tickling yet quivering tight; the man's breath was warm against her belly, his breath was warm against the crinkly hairs that sprouted between her legs, of which she was embarrassed, the fuzzy little bush at which Roy Mraz laughed. *Don't, no, please no I don't want this,* Katya was pleading, for he'd seen the little black spade tattoo on the inside of her thigh and this too he was kissing, licking with his tongue, between her legs he was licking with his tongue and sucking and Katya tried to push him away but could not, and could not raise her voice, could not protest for she was so very tired, her arms, her legs were so heavy, unresponsive to her will. Her thoughts came too slowly now to be grasped, like clouds passing so slowly overhead you can't discern their movement, and still there was, in the distance, the teasing *slap-slap-slap* of the waves. A sudden piercing sensation gripped Katya, a concentration of nerve endings like charged wires; she began to whimper, like a young child whimpering, helpless and thrashing from side to side, as if impaled, yet slowly, for she could not wake herself fully — the soft black muck of the Pine Barrens held her fast.

In a kingdom by the sea dwelt a Fair Maiden. And the King of this kingdom was agèd and yearning to die, for he had lived a very long time and was ripe to die yet feared Death, who boasted to him: "You are soon to die, old man! You are not royalty to me but just such an old man as any commoner in your kingdom — you are no one special and will fester and rot and stink like all the others." Death was an unshaven lout with a face crude as a boot, bulging bloodshot eyes, wild sprouting whiskers, warts on all his fingers, and a smell of garlic on his breath. Who was Death but an alehouse proprietor lacking all dignity!

And the agèd King was bred to dignity, vanity, and pride and could not bear so crude an execution. He was a lonely King who had outlived his wives and even his children and took little solace in the pleasures of his elderly life. And he feared there was a curse on him, that though of noble birth he was destined for a commoner's death, and such festering and rot as Death promised. And so the King had but one final request: he must die at the hand of the fairest maiden in the land, for then his death would be delicious to him, and not sordid.

So long the agèd King had dwelt in his castle high above the sea and the town below; his subjects feared him, for the King had such powers to peer into their hearts and to know them as their neighbors and even their families did not know them. But the agèd King was a wise man and a seer and took little solace in his powers, which left him chastened by melancholy and lonelier than before. In the King's troubled sleep the Fair Maiden was revealed: she who was but a child, not yet a woman, in the care of her agèd grandmother, a beautiful shining blond child, and pure of heart like no other maiden in the kingdom.

And the King's heart, which had long been brittle as stone, was rent in two, and the King woke as from a magician's enchantment, and joy and purpose filled his heart, and for the first time in many years the King wished to leave his castle and descend into the town and walk among the common people, in disguise so that they should not know him, and fall to the ground in fearful homage to him. And the King was jostled by the crowds in the town square, seeing how some persons were rude, and others were courteous; some were loud and coarse as brutes, and others were warm, sympathetic, and friendly; and the King saw that these were his subjects, and he could not judge them.

"These are my subjects. I have the power to bless."

And so the King entered the church, and knelt and prayed with the congregation; and even the priest did not recognize who had come to worship in their midst. And among the communicants appeared the Fair Maiden, exactly as she had appeared in the agèd King's dream; and the King knew her at once, and knelt before her. And the Fair Maiden shrank from him, in modesty and alarm, and ran away to her home; and the King bade his servants to seek her out and to bring her to him, to pay to the girl's grandmother whatever sum of money was required, to fetch the Fair Maiden to his castle to be the agèd King's last bride. And in his bedchamber the agèd King prayed: "She who is the Fair Maiden must come to me — the King's executioner must she be."

And so the grandmother was offered a sum of money for the Fair Maiden, and in vehement pride said no. And yet again the grandmother was offered money, a higher sum, and in vehement pride said no. And a third time the grandmother was offered money, a yet higher sum, and this time the elderly woman said yes.

And so it happened that the Fair Maiden was brought to the agèd King, and in a private ceremony in the castle they were wed by the priest, who blessed them, though the Fair Maiden, who was very young and knew little of the ways of the world, was stricken with fear of her agèd royal bridegroom, as of the opulence of the castle, and could not cease weeping; and the King vowed to her that he adored her and would never wish to harm her: "For you are my soul mate, my dear bride — no more would I wish to harm you than I would wish to harm my own soul."

And when all others were banished from their presence, and when the King and the Fair Maiden were at last alone in the King's bedchamber, the King explained to his bride that it was not an impure, carnal love for which he had wed her, but that his bride should be his executioner, that the King might thwart Death. For the King had outlived his life, and wished to die while he yet retained some measure of youthful dignity. Her reward would be great, not only wealth and property and the most exquisite jewels, but her knowledge that she had fulfilled the King's great wish, and she would be known in all the kingdom as the King's soul mate, and so revered and envied. In their bridal bed, the agèd King would lie with his arms folded across his chest, and very still, and the Fair Maiden would lie beside him, unclothed; by glimmering firelight the Fair Maiden would spread her long golden hair over the King's face, and coil it around his throat, and tighten it, and press her soft lips against his with all the force of her young body, and suck the very life from him, that the King's agèd heart would quicken, and strain, and burst in very rapture. And the King would pass from this vale of tears and strife into the next life, with no pain; his soul would expire and be released of all torment; the King would escape the crude alehouse lout Death, left thwarted outside the gates of the castle, in mud and pelting rain. In the firelit bedchamber, the Fair Maiden would summon the priest to bless her husband, and she alone would prepare his gaunt, agèd body, tenderly washing it and wrapping it in the raiments of the grave, and a final time kiss the King's cold lips and bid her royal bridegroom adieu.

And so it came to pass that the agèd King died happily in the arms of the Fair Maiden; and the Fair Maiden, who was both bride and widow on her wedding night, came to be known through all the kingdom as the King's soul mate, and revered and envied by all for the remainder of her life.

With a shudder Katya woke from her heavy, stuporous sleep. What time was it! What had happened to her! Her mouth was parched, as if she'd swallowed sand. She was lying on the sofa in a stiff and contorted posture, as if she'd fallen from a great height; beneath her the velvet cloth was bunched, and chafed against her skin. The white shawl was covering her again; someone had drawn it to her chin. Dimly she saw, seated in a chair only a few feet away, a male figure. The shade of the lamp beside him had been tilted to throw light on Katya's face and not on his own, and the panicked thought came to Katya, *He has been watching me in my sleep.*

Yet more panicked: *He has done something to me in my sleep.* "Mr. Kidder! What t-time is . . ."

Clumsily Katya tried to sit up. Something was wrong; her head seemed to swirl. She was naked beneath the shawl and — had someone lain beside her, on the sofa? While she was naked? Vaguely she remembered his arms around her, his mouth on her; her effort to throw him off, and her gradual submission; the strange tale he'd told her, as you'd tell a child at bedtime, which had sounded like a fairy tale, of an agèd King yearning to die and a Fair Maiden chosen to be his executioner . . .

Katya was shocked to see, by the mantel clock, that it was nearly 2 A.M. So late! Mr. Kidder must have put something in her drink. Must have drugged her. Half pleading, she said, "Mr. Kidder, what did you do to me? I — I feel so strange. My head is so strange. I — I want to leave now . . ."

Still Katya was very groggy and could barely sit up.

Weak as if she'd had a sudden attack of flu. Yet with maddening calmness Mr. Kidder sat in his wicker chair regarding her with his shadow-eyes, as he'd regarded her from behind his easel. There was something wrong with Mr. Kidder: the handsome ruin of a face now looked ghastly, ghoulish. Most shocking was the absence of his snowy white hair . . . In a cajoling voice he said, "Dear Katya! Juan is gone for the night, but of course I will drive you. As soon as you are ready to leave, it's back to the Mayflies, to whom you seem so perversely attached."

Katya could not bear it that Marcus Kidder was trying to make a joke of this. She was furious with him, trying to stand: "What — what did you do to me? It was more than just wine, wasn't it! Made me fall asleep, so you could do nasty things to me! I — I hate you —"

Mr. Kidder pressed a forefinger to his lips. "Katya, not so loud. This is Proxmire Street, at nearly two in the morning. I assure you, everyone else is asleep, for this is an elderly neighborhood. We do not want to attract the attention of the local police, do we? You are perfectly all right, as you must know. Dear Katya Spivak of Vineland, New Jersey, whom someone, a lusty lover I would guess, has branded as his own in the tender flesh of your thigh. Surely you are much safer with Marcus Kidder."

Katya managed to teeter to her feet. Bare feet, her toes clutching at the hardwood floor. She held the shawl against her as she willed herself to stand, not to give in to a weak sensation in her knees and sink back down on the sofa. "I can't believe you would do this to me! I trusted you! You said you l-loved me —"

Mr. Kidder protested: "Katya, of course I love you. Though knowing now more about you, yet I still love you. As I've said, you and I are soul mates, and that will never change. Frankly, I didn't intend to reveal myself to you so openly so soon. Before our bond of intimacy had deepened. But I have decided I don't want to wait much longer. As you see, I am not quite the person you thought I was." With a smile, indicating his nearly bald head, for the snowy white hair must have been a wig. Katya could see that Mr. Kidder's head was covered in a scruffy, tarnished silver down and looked shrunken, pitiable. And his eyes were the eyes of a death's-head. The vertical lines on his face seemed to have deepened, bracketing his thin-lipped mouth, which shaped itself into Marcus Kidder's familiar mock-wistful smile: "I am the agèd King, dear. You are the Fair Maiden. To be blunt, I am asking you to assist me in a very pragmatic act of . . . I believe the clinical term is euthanasia — mercy killing. Not by strangulation, nor by sucking away my breath — don't look so alarmed, dear Katya. We will be more civilized, more merciful. I have amassed a generous store of painkillers — opiates — and we will drink champagne in our bridal bed. Not immediately, my dear — but soon, I think. Once my financial affairs are in order, and on both sides we are in agreement about how you, dear Katya, will be rewarded." Mr. Kidder paused as his smile became more pained. "You would not make me beg, would you? For it is exactly as the doomed old King wished, to die in the arms of the Fair Maiden, and not at the hand of crude Death."

Katya stammered, "Th-this is a — joke, isn't it? Please, Mr. Kidder, it's a joke, right? You're laughing at me right now — aren't you?"

But Mr. Kidder wasn't laughing, just smiling. "You will have plenty of time to make a wise decision, Katya. You will not be rushed. I am utterly serious, of course. Funny Bunny is always utterly serious, even as he is a very funny bunny. And I will be true to my word to reward you generously. Before the . . . occasion, as well as after. You've learned, dear Katya, that you can trust me to pay you generously, yes?"

Katya pressed her hands against her ears. How terrible this conversation was! Her eyes flooded with tears of vexation. "I don't b-believe you, Mr. K-Kidder! You are — you are joking, aren't you! Except this is *not funny* . . ."

"Katya, on the morning we first met, I'd just come from my nephrologist's office — and just the previous day from my gastroenterologist's office. Such fancy words, eh? Pray, dear Katya, in the heedless health of youth, you will never learn what they mean. And the news was both good and not so good: after a siege of somewhere beyond eighteen months of radiation and chemotherapy, Marcus Kidder had been diagnosed as — seemingly! tentatively! — in remission. And was this good or not so good news? For if you are in remission — and not for the first time, it pains me to admit — you must live with the shadow over your head, like a black thunderhead, that there will come a time, perhaps soon — no fear, it will come — when you are no longer in remission, when you must again be strapped into zapping machines and injected with sizzling chemicals, and must endure again what you'd only just managed to endure. By which time — for time weakens us all — it may be too late to act upon your deepest wish, which is a wish that can be fulfilled only when you are strong and clear-minded and, indeed, in remission — succinctly put, not to be. 'To cease upon the midnight with no pain.' For everyone waits too long in such matters. As the agèd King knows, having seen too many others in the last grasping, gasping months of their desperate lives . . ."

Katya heard some of this. Katya heard as much as she wanted to hear of this. *He wants me to help him die. Help him kill himself. That is what he wants of me!* Desperate now to escape this stifling room, this terrible place; how trapped she felt here, drugged, paralyzed, desperate to get back to her room in the Engelhardts' house before anyone knew she was missing. Mr. Kidder was on his feet with the intention of helping Katya walk, for her legs were unsteady, but Katya shoved at the strange bald man, whom she hardly knew — "No! Don't touch me!" — made her way, stumbling, to the bathroom, locked the door behind her, and hurriedly dressed, seeing in the mirror a girl's pale, sickly, frightened face. Yes, but Katya was angry too, Katya was damned angry, fumbling with her clothing, taking no heed that she'd pulled the top on backward, kicking her feet into her sandals; she was furious and trembling, unlocking the door and pushing past the disgusting old man hovering just outside, damned old baldie-head, scruffy baldie-head, like her own grandfather Spivak he was, an elderly sick pitiable man yet like a vulture, the hungry eyes, the disgusting mouth sucking at her energy. In the street Katya wouldn't have given such a man a second glance; on Ocean Avenue that morning, if he hadn't been wearing his snowy white wig and hadn't been dressed so elegantly and carried a cane and had such an upright posture, she'd have turned away from him at once, hurried little Tricia and the baby away from him, for here was Death plucking at her wrist, here was Death wanting to embrace her. Katya threw him off, threw off his hand from her wrist; such curses sprang from her mouth as she'd been hearing for much of her life in Vineland, *Fuck you, the hell with you, goddamn you bastard leave me alone,* as she fumbled to snatch up her bag, ignored the old man's apologies, his pleas, his offer to pay her, *goddamn.* Katya was too furious and too agitated to remain in this terrible place another moment, but pushed out the door, outside and into the night. At once the fresh chill ocean air revived her, and the smell of the ocean, the angry *slap-slap-slap* of the surf; she was running to the front gate, and behind her Marcus Kidder's uplifted voice: "Think it over, Katya! The offer — the King — will be waiting for you."

24

Will not, I will not. God damn him to hell — he has no right.
  Killing is a sin! He can't make me do this.
  He touched me. Did things to me in my sleep.
  I don't love him. I could not love an old, sick, dying man.

25

AT THE YACHT CLUB beach in the presence of Tricia Engelhardt, whose endearingly clumsy surf-wading Katya was super-
vising, Katya managed to score from the lanky nineteen-year-old
lifeguard, receiving from his hand a single mashed joint and a
single OxyContin with the promise from Katya that they'd hook
up Friday night at a club in town, and Katya said *Sure!* in her
nerved-up state, turning away before thinking to say *And thanks!*
over her shoulder as the dark-tanned boy, whose name she'd
have to think hard to recall — Dave? Dan? — stared after her the
way a hungry carnivore might gaze after something smaller and
warm-blooded. Later, back at the Engelhardts', fortified by the
OxyContin, Katya dared to call Roy Mraz at her uncle Fritzie's
garage in Vineland, an act that might have the effect of tossing a
lighted match — casually, recklessly — into dried and desiccated
underbrush, though telling herself *It's a roll of the dice* and the
decision was out of her hands, as Katya's father used to say with a
smile and a shrug: *You roll the dice but how the damned dice fall
is out of your power,* and Jude Spivak was right. And Katya was
thinking that Roy Mraz wouldn't be at the garage in Vineland
any longer, he'd have moved on by now, and she would be spared
what she was going to do, for part of her was frightened of her
own rage, but there came Roy's voice, abrupt and startling in her
ear — *Hey, Katya? That you?* — and Katya felt faint, as if the oxy-
gen in her brain had been shut off, as if Roy Mraz had prankishly
shoved his hand into her chest to squeeze her beating heart with
his fingers; and there came words pouring from her in the voice
of a hurt and vindictive child: *There is this man here! In Bayhead*

Harbor! He drugged me, put his hands on me, asked me to do a terrible thing! A disgusting thing! He's a rich man, a rich old man here in Bayhead. And Roy broke in, laughing: *Whoa! What the hell, Katz? What're you telling me?* And Katya's throat shut, she stammered and could only just beg: *Help me, Roy. Come here and help me, Roy, I'm so afraid.*

And so it was, tossing the lighted match.

"My cousin is driving up from Vineland, Mrs. Engelhardt. After I put Tricia to bed, I have to go out for a while."

It was a statement, not a plea, nor even a request. Seeing the look in Katya's face of something ravaged and torn, Mrs. Engelhardt must have considered asking her sixteen-year-old nanny if something serious was wrong, but just said, with a prissy frown, "Don't stay out too late, please! We have a busy day tomorrow."

That night he came for her in a steel-colored SUV that resembled a military vehicle. Its chassis rode high on oversized black tires and on its rust-flecked front grille were the letters RAM-CHARGER. Anxious and excited, Katya climbed up into the passenger's seat, and Roy Mraz leaned over and grabbed her and kissed her hard and pushed her from him, baring stained shark teeth in a laugh. "All growed up, eh?"

This was the first time Katya had seen Roy Mraz in more than eighteen months. The first time since Roy had been released on parole from the State Facility for Men at Glassboro, where he'd been sentenced to three years on counts of aggravated assault, possession of an unlicensed firearm, resisting arrest. Roy had been involved in drugs too, but he hadn't had drugs in his possession when he'd been arrested. Close beside Roy Mraz now, Katya felt a stab of alarm, apprehension. Roy was older; his features were coarser, his jaws covered in dark stubble. His bluish black hair was shaved brutally close to his skull on the sides of his head and grew long, wiry, and springy at the crown in what might have been south Jersey biker style. Katya saw a two-inch scar above Roy's left eye that she'd never seen before. Roy had gained weight in prison, muscled flesh in his torso and shoulders and neck; on his beefy right forearm Katya saw a smudged tattoo of something like a flaming dagger. He wore stained khakis, biker's boots, a blue and yellow Eagles jersey. His driving was aggressive and erratic, and when he stopped for a red light on Ocean Avenue, he pulled Katya to him again and kissed her as he'd kissed her before, hard, and quick, and no sentiment in it, a kiss that was a warning. Swiftly he ran his hands over her, up inside her shirt, squeezing her ribs, her breasts in a cotton bra, and the flesh at the small of her back as a belligerent blind man might do, to establish her identity to him and his claim over her.

"Missed you, baby! A lot."

With an air of reproach Roy Mraz spoke, as if daring Katya to believe him.

As if I'd miss you, my kid cousin. All the girls and women a guy like me has, who are crazy for him.

Along Ocean Avenue Roy drove them out of the affluent Village of Bayhead Harbor south along the highway into a countryside of small ranch houses, trailer parks, and mini-malls and at last into a stretch of sand dunes, sand grasses, scrub trees growing low against the ground. Briny ocean air tinged with a smell of dead and decaying fish rushed at their faces. Roy was smoking a joint and he passed it to Katya, who took it eagerly, for she was very nervous, had no idea what Roy Mraz would do, no more (maybe) than Roy Mraz himself knew, for Roy Mraz and his brothers and friends were guys who behaved impulsively, though sometimes by calculation, and you had to wonder which was worse. Katya was recalling how Roy Mraz had taken her out when she'd been scarcely fourteen years old and had flirted with him, must've been that Katya had been one of those girls who'd been crazy for Roy Mraz without knowing much about him, and he'd laughed at her, saying, *It won't hurt, Katya, not much,* and, by the time it was too late for Katya to change her mind, *Just this first time, maybe.* Katya had not wanted to think how this past year in Vineland she'd been hearing rumors that Roy Mraz had done things in prison — or maybe things had been done to Roy Mraz in prison — but Katya hadn't known what these things were alleged to be. (From her grandfather Spivak, who'd been a prison guard at Glassboro for more than thirty years, Katya had an idea.) And it was said — Katya was remembering only now, as if mists were lifting slowly, revealing a devastated landscape — that this young man who was, or was not, her blood relative had helped two older men rob a gas station when he'd been nineteen, and when the proprietor rushed at them with a baseball bat, one of the men panicked and shot him several times in the chest and he'd died on the floor of the gas station on the outskirts of Atlantic City, and if Roy Mraz hadn't been the one who'd fired the gun, he'd been an accomplice. *Felony murder,* this was. Katya was in a speeding SUV with an individual whom she scarcely knew who had committed *felony murder,* and yet . . . she must have wanted this, for she'd called Roy Mraz, and she'd summoned him to her, and he was here.

How many crimes, how many murders go unsolved, unpunished? This was not TV or movies or mystery novels in which crimes were always solved and criminals brought to justice, this was actual life. *What a man is sentenced for, what a man does time for, is never all that a man has done,* Katya had heard adults say with grim satisfaction. Such knowledge made her shiver, for it could not be refuted.

In a desolate place off Route 37, Roy parked the steel-colored Ramcharger. At the base of a raggedy sand dune he kissed Katya with his big bared teeth, called her *Katz,* called her *baby,* said he couldn't believe how hot she was, last time he'd seen her she was just a kid, Jesus he'd missed her! Pulling impatiently at her clothes as a child might tug in frustration at something that did not yield immediately, and so quickly Katya removed her pretty things before Roy Mraz ripped them; within seconds then Roy Mraz was lying on her, the weight of his large heated body on her made it difficult for Katya to breathe, and there was Roy pushing himself deep inside Katya, grunting with the effort, hard and quick and without sentiment, and there was Roy's grimacing mouth pressed against Katya's mouth, hurting the tender flesh of her lips, nothing tender in Roy Mraz's kiss as there had been in Mr. Kidder's kisses, but Katya was not going to think of Marcus Kidder now, Katya wished never to think of Marcus Kidder in this way. Not ever wishing to think, *But he is the one who loves you, not this one! Mr. Kidder is the only one who knows you and loves you or will ever love you in all your life.* Gamely Katya tried to embrace Roy Mraz's sweaty muscled shoulders, tried to kiss him and murmur to him words to please and to placate. It disturbed her that Roy's lovemaking was rapid and impersonal, as if he were hardly aware of Katya Spivak and only of a pliant female body into which he pumped himself, panting and grunting, still with that air of impatience as the back of Katya's head was struck against the hard-packed sand beneath them — Oh! it hurt. *Oh, oh!* Katya bit her lip to keep from crying out, tried not to sob so that the man would think it must be a sexual sensation she was feeling and not chafing and pain, and even now she was thinking, *Do I know him? Do I want this?* until finally it was over and Roy rolled off her, heavy and leaden in the aftermath of passion like a corpse; and for some time they lay side by side, not touching, panting, stunned, like strangers struck down by a single catastrophic blow in a litter-strewn desolate place off Route 37, and like a child's cry heard at a distance, the thought came to Katya: *But maybe he will love me now?*

Roy had rented a room on the highway, he said. He'd be staying the night — maybe two nights — and Katya could stay with him and get back to the place where she worked early, before they missed her; or maybe, if things worked out right, Katya could quit the damn job, and the hell with it. Roy was sitting up and brushing sand from the dark curly wires that sprouted from his chest, fumbling for a cigarette out of a pocket of his khaki pants, tossed down nearby. He lit the cigarette, exhaled smoke in a luxurious stream, and said, with a mean-boy smile, "This guy you told me about on the phone. Who 'did things' to you? He's rich, you said? How rich?"

26

Roll the dice, see what happens. Why the hell not?

Must've been a kind of boastfulness — she'd directed Roy Mraz
into the Village of Bayhead Harbor, wanting to impress him.
Heard Roy Mraz whistle thinly through his teeth, muttering *Shit!*
and *Fuck!* and *Jeez-uz!*, seeing what he could of the dazzling
oceanside houses and the small sea of yachts and sailboats in the
lighted marina and then into the historic district and along leafy
Proxmire Street lined with tall sculpted smooth-barked plane trees
that glimmered by moonlight. And by this time they'd gotten high
together smoking ice in the Sand Dollar Motel — granular crystal meth that Roy had scored from his Atlantic City dealer. (And
was Roy himself dealing, on a small scale, in Vineland? From remarks he made to Katya, and a hint that he wouldn't be working
at Fritzie's garage much longer, this seemed likely.) (And would
Roy take Katya with him if he left Vineland? High on ice, every
other word uttered with a breathy giggle, Katya could plausibly
think, *Maybe*.) And so, directing Roy Mraz in the steel-colored
military vehicle along genteel Proxmire Street. Liking how Roy
stared scowling at the private homes the size of small hotels that
were tauntingly visible through openings in the privet hedges,
and feeling a thrill of pride when Roy whistled, saying, "You've
been in *there*?" when Katya pointed out Mr. Kidder's house. Roy
braked the Ramcharger to a stop at the curb and leaned out the
window to peer at the near-darkened shingleboard house, which
by moonlight was like a house in a children's picture book of some
bygone time, and like nothing in all of Vineland, New Jersey. And
Katya said, Yes, sure, she'd been inside.

A tingling sensation inside her head. That sensation of some-thing finely vibrating, electric current rippling through it, you wanted to think it wasn't the drug but your truest self, your self that wasn't fearful of anything and did not frankly give a shit about anything except *Now! now now* and not instead *But I don't want this really — do I? This is a mistake — isn't it?* as Roy sat brooding and grimacing, staring at Marcus Kidder's beautiful house from a distance of less than fifty feet, and Katya's thoughts came drift-ing at her in misshapen cartoon balloons that, if you grabbed at them, would slip from your fingers and drift away. Roy was asking Katya how she'd hooked up with this guy, and Katya told him in a voice of naive earnestness that his name was Marcus Kidder and he was a famous man in Bayhead Harbor and he knew everyone because he belonged to all the private clubs. He must have rec-ognized the Engelhardt children when he saw them with Katya in the park; and so it happened that Mr. Kidder invited them to tea-time at his house, where they sat on a terrace overlooking the ocean; and Mr. Kidder showed Katya paintings on the walls of his studio, for it turned out that he was an artist; and he asked her if she'd like to pose for him sometime, and so — "What kind of artist?" Roy interrupted suspiciously, and Katya said, as if pro-testing, "A real artist! A serious artist like you'd see in a museum. And Mr. Kidder is a writer, too, he's done children's books that are in the library," and Roy said, "So this old guy paid you, eh? To pose for him?" and Katya said, "Yes," and Roy said, sneer-ing, "With your clothes on or off?" and Katya laughed, saying, "Mostly on," and Roy said, "What'd he do to you, Katz — did he fuck you?" and Katya said, her voice now lowered, less certain, "He put s-something in a drink, and I—I guess I passed out. I don't know all that he did," and Roy laughed harshly, as if in dis-gust at her, and Katya was confused, not knowing what she'd said or meant to say or why her mouth was so dry, why she was swal-lowing compulsively as if granules of sand had gotten into her mouth.

For some minutes Roy Mraz sat silently contemplating the shingleboard house glimmering in the moonlight, visible in the opening in the privet hedge for the circular driveway. It was then that headlights moved suddenly upon them from an oncoming vehicle and Katya tasted panic — what if this was a Bayhead Harbor police cruiser, what if they were discovered and arrested for trespassing, they could be arrested, couldn't they? in this neighborhood, at this hour? But the vehicle with the blinding headlights passed by and was revealed to be an ordinary car. Abruptly then Roy squeezed Katya's bare knee hard, hard enough to make her wince, as if he'd decided something and it was a decision he felt good about. Saying, "So you took money from this Kidder, baby. So whatever he did to you, he paid you. So he won't mind paying you a little more."

Katya swallowed hard. Katya shivered, and laid her hand over Roy Mraz's heavy hand on her knee. Katya whispered, *Yes.*

Following which, things happened swiftly.

Not all of which Katya Spivak would recall afterward.

Though she would recall calling Marcus Kidder from a pay phone outside a 7-Eleven store in Bayhead Harbor as Roy Mraz leaned over her, listening: "Mr. K-Kidder? It's me, Katya? I — I'd like to come back to see you, Mr. Kidder, like you said —" in a faint, halting voice, and at the other end of the line there was a startled silence followed by the surprised and elated voice of Marcus Kidder. "Why, Katya! My dear! I've been sitting here feeling lonely and sorry for myself and not daring to hope that you'd call. Can you come tonight?" Katya bit her lip, reluctant to answer, but Roy had heard, Roy gripped and squeezed her shoulder, and so Katya said, "Y-yes, as soon as I — I can. I need to do some things here and then I —" as the receiver fell from her slippery fingers and Roy Mraz caught it swinging at the end of its cord, wiped the receiver clean with a wadded tissue, and hung it up.

It was eleven-fifteen of that humid August night in Bayhead Harbor when Roy Mraz and Katya Spivak returned in the Ram-

[146]

charger to 17 Proxmire Street. Katya saw that outside lights had been switched on. And there stood a white-haired figure waiting on the front stoop for her, diminished by the size of the house behind him and by distorting nighttime shadows. While Roy waited behind the privet hedge, Katya hurried up the flagstone path and Mr. Kidder came forward to greet her eagerly in an embrace, brushing his lips against her cheek; for a long tremulous moment he held her tight. "Darling Katya! My love! I thought I'd lost my soul mate forever." How Roy Mraz would sneer at these extravagant words if he heard them! Katya felt a pang of pity for Marcus Kidder, stepping back from his embrace to see that he gazed upon her with watery adoring eyes. In preparation for her visit he'd shaved, and he smelled of fresh cologne; he'd changed into linen trousers and a shirt of some fine fabric. Covering his stubbled bald head was the snowy white wig, which seemed to Katya the most piteous thing about Marcus Kidder.

Eagerly Mr. Kidder was speaking to Katya, who could not manage more than a few mumbled words to him.

Inside the house, in the dimly lighted foyer, Mr. Kidder was just shutting the front door when Roy Mraz shoved it rudely open and pushed his way inside. As Mr. Kidder saw Roy Mraz with his belligerent young face and excited eyes and his dark hair shaved at the sides of his head, he must have known what was going to happen.

Tersely Roy said, "Inside, Kidder. And keep your mouth shut."

Katya turned aside guiltily. She could not meet Mr. Kidder's stricken gaze. She heard the astonished old man ask Roy who he was, why was he here, how dare he push his way inside this house, and she heard Roy say insolently that Katya was his cousin and Katya was only fifteen years old — "She says you drugged her and raped her, you sick bastard." And Mr. Kidder protested, "I — I never did such a thing — I l-love Katya, I would never —" and Roy said, shoving at Mr. Kidder, "She told me everything! She called me! Dirty old pervert, you are going to pay."

Confused, badly frightened, Mr. Kidder appealed to Katya to explain to Roy Mraz that he hadn't hurt her — "You know, Katya, that I didn't, don't you? Katya, tell him" — and in that instant saw in Katya's face that she'd betrayed him. Of course, it had to be Katya who'd betrayed him; it was Katya who'd brought this furious young man into Mr. Kidder's house. Roy was saying that if Mr. Kidder didn't give them what they deserved they were going to the Bayhead police; and Mr. Kidder recovered enough of his poise to say that he wasn't going to be blackmailed; and Roy said mockingly, "Yeah? You won't? Then give my cousin what you owe her, you old shit." High on ice, Roy was flush-faced with heat and his forehead oozed sweat; he'd sweated through his Eagles jersey and stank of his body. Yet Katya saw that Roy had had the presence of mind to put on leather gloves, and this detail made her sick with apprehension. *So he won't leave prints. Whatever he does to Mr. Kidder, he has prepared for.*

Bravely, Mr. Kidder told Roy Mraz that if he and Katya left now, he wouldn't report them to the police, and Roy laughed at him, shoving him in the chest with the flat of his hand, demanding money: "And whatever else you got, we deserve. Silverware, gold things, all kinds of expensive crap — you owe us, fucker." Mr. Kidder's face had drained of blood, he was shaky on his feet; he was pressing his hand against his chest as if he were in pain. With shocked and despairing eyes he looked at Katya, who stammered guiltily, "Roy? M-Maybe we should just leave? He's sorry for what he —" Roy struck Katya with the flat of his hand, not hard, but hard enough to silence her. "Shut your mouth, for Christ's sake. You crazy? We're not leaving until this fucker pays us."

Roy forced Mr. Kidder to lead him into the rear of the house, to Mr. Kidder's studio, where he kept financial records in a large antique desk. Here on the walls were the portraits of Marcus Kidder's female subjects in gentle pastels, and for a moment Katya felt a shudder of dread that one of Marcus Kidder's portraits of her might be hanging among them for Roy Mraz to mock.

Roy demanded that Mr. Kidder give him money, and Mr. Kidder was protesting that he hadn't any money in the house, never kept money in the house, only a few bills in his wallet; and Roy took his wallet from him, opened it, and yanked out a handful of bills and several small plastic cards, moving so jerkily, so clumsily, that some of the bills slipped from Roy's hand, and a small plastic card — not a credit card, Katya saw, but a card for the Bayhead Harbor public library. Roy then forced Mr. Kidder to take out his checkbook from one of the desk drawers and to make out a check for ten thousand dollars to Katya Spivak — "You owe Katya, and you know it." Roy pushed Mr. Kidder down into his desk chair, and Mr. Kidder fumbled for a pen, his hand shaking; as Roy crouched over him, Mr. Kidder began to make out a check, but his hand swerved, and the check was ruined; and Roy said, "You did that on purpose! Fuck you, old bastard, pervert, you've been lucky so far I haven't broken your face, filthy son of a bitch, putting your hands on my girl cousin, your dirty-old-man dick in my girl cousin, know what that is? Statutory rape — any kind of sex with a minor. She's only fifteen, did you know that, you son of a bitch? It's statutory rape — and you gave her drugs, some kind of sleeping pill, she said. You kept her here, that's kidnapping — adduction — you can get a life sentence for shit like that. Better make that twenty thousand, you filthy piece of shit." Roy was sweating profusely, and his eyes glittered crazily with the glassy sheen of the fossil flowers, crystalline flowers displayed in elegant vases and urns that Roy had only begun to notice; as if such beauty tormented him, he struck at random at the glass flowers with his fists — "What're these freaky things? Jeez-zus" — and with a sweep of his arm he cleared the fireplace mantel, glass flowers fell and shattered on the floor, and Mr. Kidder feebly protested: "You are a barbarian! You have no right! Get out of my house!" As Katya looked on in horror, Mr. Kidder dared to seize a carved sculpture on his desk and swing it at Roy Mraz, striking Roy in the chest. Roy laughed, incensed, and attacked the old man mercilessly with his fists: "You old fuck! What d'you think you're doing!" As Roy Mraz beat Marcus Kidder, Katya tried to intervene, tried to stop Roy's fists, but Roy threw her off — "What the fuck, Katya! Get away." Something struck Katya on the side of the head, near her left temple; she staggered and fell against one of the wicker chairs. For a moment she was blinded, as if concussed. Somehow Roy had hit her face, and her face was bleeding, and on the floor was Marcus Kidder, dazed, dripping blood, trying to rise to his knees as Roy cursed him, and laughed at him, and kicked him. Mr. Kidder was bleeding from a deep cut above his right eye and cuts at his nose and mouth; his breathing was labored and painful. Roy had no pity for him, now kicking him in the ribs and in the stomach, and, as the stricken elderly man tried to shield himself from the young man's blows, like a curling worm, in the back. Katya screamed for Roy to stop. She'd never seen so much blood from a head wound, dark rushing streams of blood; Mr. Kidder's eyes shone with terror, then glazed over. His bleeding mouth went slack and he lay still. Katya was begging Roy: "Let me call for help, Roy, for an ambulance, what if he dies?" and Roy cursed her and shoved her from him. "This is fucked up, goddamn you. This wasn't supposed to happen, you stupid cunt, this is fucked up . . ." Roy was opening desk drawers, spilling papers, manila files, financial records onto the floor. Katya approached a wall phone with the idea of dialing 911 before Roy saw her, but he saw her, dragged her away, and slapped her, deciding then that they had better leave, that someone in the neighborhood might have heard them. He pulled Katya out of the studio, where Mr. Kidder lay moaning on the floor beside the desk amid a glitter of broken glass, and along the hall to the front of the house and to the front door, which all this while had been left ajar, so that anyone might have walked in. "Jesus! Is this fucked up." Roy laughed harshly, as if he'd never seen anything so funny.

And in the SUV, driving away, Roy continued to laugh and to mutter to himself, and Katya pleaded with him, "Roy, please — let me call an ambulance from a pay phone, they won't know who made the call, please Roy, what if Mr. Kidder dies —" and Roy told her to shut up. And Katya dared to persist, for she could not bear it that she'd betrayed Marcus Kidder, she loved Marcus Kidder and she'd betrayed him and was leaving him now to die. She was crying, pulling at Roy's arm as Roy drove them along the residential street lined with glimmering and unearthly plane trees, and Roy said in a cold, furious voice, "You've got a thing for that old pervert, don't you! You and him. Jesus, is that disgusting. You liked him fucking you, eh? If he could? How'd he do it? Old bastard old enough to be your grandfather. Crazy like your father — know what he did? Jude Spivak? Instead of getting the hell out before they killed him, he thought he could make it up to these guys he owed money to — serious money — and he's dumped out in the Barrens, which everybody knows, or can figure, except you Spivaks." Katya stared at Roy Mraz, at Roy Mraz's face, blunt as a boot, sweaty and smirking. She was uncertain what she'd heard: her father was dead? Jude Spivak was dead? And his body dumped? In the Barrens, his body *dumped*? All this time that Katya had been waiting for him to return to her, he'd been dead, and everyone in Vineland had known . . .

Katya took hold of the door handle and turned it; she had the door open before Roy could stop her. Roy braked the vehicle, cursed, and reached for her, but in his disgust with her changed his mind, and as the passenger door swung open, Roy shoved her out while the SUV was moving at about fifteen miles an hour. And Katya fell out, and onto the pavement, and lay there stunned, a high-pitched ringing in her ear, as Roy Mraz drove away, tires squealing.

So quickly this happened. As Katya lay confused and unsure of her surroundings, the glassy-sharp clarity of the meth high, which was a purely visual clarity, rapidly faded. Katya felt now the heaviness of sorrow, loss. *All along, he was dead! And I have betrayed Mr. Kidder, who is the only one who loves me.*

Wincing with pain, Katya picked herself up from the pavement. No idea where she was, where Roy had dumped her. She was in terror that Roy would return and drag her back into the SUV and out in the sand dunes, what Roy Mraz might do to her with his fists and feet in biker's boots . . . A block ahead was a lighted street; Katya began limping in that direction. Both her knees were scraped, bleeding, scraped raw on the pavement. Her clothing, so carefully chosen to impress Roy Mraz, was torn and bloodstained. Her mouth and right eye felt swollen. Through a haze of pain, Katya recognized the street ahead: Meridian, which intersected with Ocean Avenue. She knew where she was now, more or less. The Engelhardts' house on New Liberty Street was less than a mile away. At this hour of a weekday night, Mrs. Engelhardt would probably be asleep.

On Meridian, beside a darkened Sunoco station, was an outdoor phone booth, to which Katya hurriedly limped, shrinking into the shadows when traffic passed near. In the phone booth she lifted the receiver and heard the dial tone and dialed 911, and when a female dispatcher answered Katya said in a rapid lowered voice, "On Proxmire Street — 17 Proxmire Street — a man has been hurt at the back of the house — a man is bleeding, and needs an ambulance —"

The dispatcher asked who was calling. Katya said *No one!* and quickly hung up the receiver.

27

If he dies, I am to blame.

And whatever happens to me, I will deserve.

There followed then days in succession dreamlike and as charged with tension as those swollen and bruise-colored cumulus clouds massing above the Atlantic Ocean, blown inland by a chill northeast wind. Sleepless and guilt-racked, Katya waited to hear the news that Marcus Kidder had died, and waited for police officers to come for Katya Spivak.

Waiting for a loud rapping on the door of the Engelhardt house overlooking the boat channel and Mr. Engelhardt's dazzling white Chris-Craft yacht. Waiting for the morning to be disturbed, rent in two. And Lorraine Engelhardt might answer the door expecting a woman friend, and if Katya was in another room with Tricia or with the baby she would hear men's voices and she would hear Mrs. Engelhardt say in a startled voice, *Who? The girl who works for us? Why, what do you want with her — ?*

Beyond this Katya didn't allow herself to think.

Beyond this her thoughts dissolved in remorse, regret.

For all of Bayhead Harbor was shocked by the news: the "home invasion" on Proxmire Street, the "attempted robbery," the "brutal, senseless beating" of the prominent Bayhead Harbor summer resident Marcus Kidder. In local newspapers, on local TV, repeatedly it was reported how Mr. Kidder, sixty-eight years old, living by himself in one of the "oldest oceanside" houses on "historic" Proxmire Street, seemed to have been "taken by surprise" in his home in the late evening; seemed to have struggled with his assailant or assailants before being "savagely" beaten and left bleeding and unconscious on the floor of his studio. By ambulance the injured man had been driven to the nearest intensive-care facility, at the University of Pennsylvania Medical School in Philadelphia, fifty miles away; there, he had not yet regained consciousness and was listed "in critical condition." Katya dreaded hearing that Marcus Kidder had died. Yet Katya dreaded hearing that Marcus Kidder had regained consciousness. Numbly thinking, *He will give them my name. That is what I deserve.*

In the Engelhardts' household, these dreamlike days, her head racked with pain and her eyes, behind dark-tinted glasses, brimming with moisture, Katya waited. For here was a throw of the dice, utterly out of her control.

"Kat-cha? Why're you sad? Kat-cha, don't cry." Anxiously Tricia Engelhardt snuggled into Katya's arms as Katya became distracted in the midst of reading to the little girl from one of her picture books. Katya wiped at her eyes and gave Tricia a quick kiss. "Kat-cha isn't sad or crying, Kat-cha is just thinking how she will miss you, and little Kevin, after Labor Day."

Tricia crinkled her nose and shook her head vigorously. No, no! It was bad to think of "after Labor Day," when Tricia would be starting preschool, back in Saddle River.

Katya had to wonder what, after Labor Day, would be Katya Spivak's life.

If Marcus Kidder died, Katya would be an accomplice to a murder. *Felony homicide*, it was.

Yet she could not go to police, she could not confess her part in the crime. She dared not provide police with Roy Mraz's name; she was terrified of what he might do to her, or to her family in Vineland.

A wildness came over her. Katya wanted to go to Mr. Kidder, to see him in his hospital bed. To beg forgiveness!

She did love him, she thought. Yet she had betrayed him.

Such remorse would be her secret. As over her bruised face Katya wore makeup for several days following Roy's attack. On the morning after the beating she'd wakened stiff and throbbing with pain, had had to drag herself from her bed in the nanny's quarters, where she'd fallen without removing her clothes, hurriedly showered and washed her hair and brushed her hair and arranged it to fall partly over her face to hide her swollen and discolored right eye. She wore dark-tinted glasses, and white cord slacks to hide her lacerated knees. Her hand shook as she applied flesh-colored makeup as thick as putty, which gave her an eerily composed, masklike look. Walking, she made an effort to resist wincing and limping. When sharp-eyed Mrs. Engelhardt saw and asked Katya what had happened, Katya said with an embarrassed laugh that she'd walked into the bathroom door in her room, in the dark — "It must have been a dream — I thought I was at home. But it doesn't hurt at all, really." So convincingly Katya spoke, Mrs. Engelhardt seemed to believe her, or to wish to believe her. "If you'd like to see a doctor, Katya, I can drive you," Mrs. Engelhardt said. "And I'll pay for it, dear. That's a nasty cut on your mouth."

Katya was deeply moved that Lorraine Engelhardt spoke so kindly to her. In these waning days of August, when Labor Day loomed near.

"You are sure, Katya, aren't you, that no one has hurt you? A boy, or a . . ." Mrs. Engelhardt's voice faltered; Katya had never seen the woman so distressed. Blood rushed into Katya's face as she realized, *She thinks I'm pregnant. She's anxious that the father might be her husband. That's my secret!*

Katya assured Mrs. Engelhardt that there was nothing to reveal.

As in a fairy tale, endings can come abruptly. And unexpectedly.

For on the morning following this exchange, Katya heard on the Engelhardts' kitchen TV, as she was feeding stewed apricots to the baby in his highchair, that Marcus Kidder had not only regained consciousness the previous day in the Philadelphia hospital, after five days in a coma, but he'd been able to describe his assailants to Bayhead Harbor police: the men who'd broken into his home to beat and rob him had been two Caucasian males in their mid-twenties, strangers he was certain he had never seen before but believed he could identify if he ever saw them again.

Two Caucasian males. Strangers!

There was Marcus Kidder on TV in closeup, in film footage of some years ago, being honored at a local gathering. Through the roaring in her ears Katya could barely make out the newscaster's words. How youthful Mr. Kidder was looking, graciously shaking hands with a female librarian who was presenting him with a plaque of some kind; how tall he was, how dignified his posture, how beautiful his head of snowy white hair . . . Katya stared, entranced, a spoonful of baby food in her hand, until the husky Engelhardt baby began to rock dangerously in his highchair and flail his little fists in hunger.

In this way Katya Spivak was given to know that Marcus Kidder had forgiven her.

28

IT WAS TWO EVENINGS before Katya's departure from Bayhead Harbor, the day before Labor Day, just twelve days following the assault on Marcus Kidder, that Mr. Kidder's driver came for her.

Katya was in Harbor Park with the Engelhardt children. Feeding geese for what would be the final time that summer.

How melancholy Katya was feeling. How heavy-hearted, on the eve of her departure. She would never see the Engelhardts again, she knew; her mother had warned her against becoming attached to strangers' children, and yet it had happened, Katya felt almost a kind of love for three-year-old Tricia, who had nearly learned to read under her tutelage, or at least to read certain of her picture books, and for Tricia's baby brother, who fussed and fretted less in his nanny's arms than he did in his mother's. For Katya knew that children inhabit a heightened present tense: they forget quickly. Within a day or two the baby would have utterly forgotten Katya Spivak, who'd fed, bathed, dressed, and cuddled him all summer; within a few weeks Tricia would have forgotten the girl who'd introduced her to Funny Bunny and his friends and had encouraged her to draw with colored pencils.

With her own colored pencils and sketchpad, Katya was trying to capture a poignant scene in the park: young children, geese with wide flapping wings and outstretched necks, the placid surface of the small lake nearby . . . But there was too much commotion and noise; Katya couldn't concentrate. One after another of the sketches Katya tried were disappointing to her; she tore out the pages and crumpled them in her hand. Why had Mr. Kidder encouraged Katya Spivak to think that she had talent? *Without Mr. Kidder, I am nothing.*

The most recent news was that Marcus Kidder had returned to Bayhead Harbor. He'd been discharged from the hospital into the care of a private nurse, unless the "private nurse" was only Mrs. Bee. For all Katya knew, Mrs. Bee was in fact a private nurse. Katya would never see Mr. Kidder again, and Katya would never see Roy Mraz again. (A few days after the beating, when she'd been waiting for Bayhead Harbor police to arrest her, Katya had called her sister Lisle to ask about Roy and been told that so far as Lisle knew, Roy Mraz had moved away from Vineland. He'd stopped work at Fritzie's garage, and no one seemed to know where he was, not even the young divorced woman with the two-year-old son whom Roy had been seeing for much of the summer.)

Katya was thinking these thoughts, which made her colored pencils falter against the stiff white paper, as if they'd lost all their magic, when there came to her, quietly from behind, Mr. Kidder's driver, Juan. "Miss, you must come with me. Mr. Kidder is awaiting you now."

Katya, astonished, turned to see the driver. For here the man stood in his dark chauffeur's uniform, white shirt and dark tie, dark visored cap, dark-tinted glasses. Politely he spoke, with the barest hint of a smile.

Katya stammered, "No! I can't. I have the children . . ."

And politely again Juan spoke, in his soft, lightly accented voice: "Mr. Kidder wishes to see you, miss. You will come with me now, please."

There was another nanny seated on a bench close by, a friendly young Hispanic woman who cared for the children of a neighbor of Mrs. Engelhardt, whom Katya had come to know from the park and the beach. Apologetically Katya asked the woman if she would do Katya a favor and take the Engelhardt children back with her to New Liberty Street, to Mrs. Engelhardt, and the young woman said, surprised, yes, of course she would.

Seeing how Juan stood a few feet away from Katya Spivak in his black chauffeur's uniform, waiting.

In this way Katya was taken back to 17 Proxmire Street.

On this warm, gusty day in late summer, in Bayhead Harbor.

Sand was blown along the roadway, against the tinted windows of the gleaming black Lincoln Town Car, stinging Katya's eyes and making them water though the windows were shut tight. The journey from Harbor Park to 17 Proxmire Street could not have taken more than five minutes, and yet it seemed much longer. Katya was having difficulty making out what passed before her eyes as in a film in which action has been speeded up, or slowed to the point of immobility. It seemed as if Juan was driving fast, for Katya had to clutch at the armrest beside her; she felt her head spin, as it had when she'd given in to Roy Mraz, to smoke crystal meth with him; she felt a dazed sense of detachment from her body, as when, as a young child, she'd sometimes awakened to such a sensation in her bed, opening her eyes, panicked, to see the ceiling spinning above her, and she was unable to move or to call for help. A terrible heart-straining effort was required to summon the strength to call for help — *Mommy! Daddy!* But it was rare that anyone heard.

As through our lives such sensations overcome us. Springing out of nowhere to threaten our souls with extinction but then, as abruptly as they've appeared, they disappear.

Or so we wish to think.

Katya was staring at the tall privet hedge that ran beside the street. Taller than she remembered, as Proxmire Street was wider and more desolate than she remembered, for the mansion-sized houses were barely visible from the street and were at a considerable distance from one another. Katya saw that the privet hedge was the boundary of something: beyond the hedge, you were forbidden entry. You were forbidden to trespass. Yet the gleaming black Lincoln Town Car with its powerful, near-silent engine turned into the driveway at 17 Proxmire Street and approached the house effortlessly, as if floating. And how large Mr. Kidder's house was, how stately and beautiful the old, weathered shingle-board and the slate roof and the several chimneys made of aged, softened brick that glowed warmly in the sun; for though the sky had darkened, as bulbous, rain-heavy cumulus clouds were being blown inland, passing close to the tops of the gigantic plane trees, yet there were bright patches of sunshine that moved swiftly across Katya's field of vision as if by design.

The flagstone path, the vivid green of the slightly overgrown grass, thistle weeds like spikes sprouting in the flowerbeds . . .

"Miss, come with me. Master has been expecting you." There was Mrs. Bee standing on the front stoop of the house in her white nylon uniform, tight-girdled, with a frowning smile and quivering jowls.

Shyly Katya approached Mr. Kidder's housekeeper. It was surprising to her that the older woman so firmly took her hand, for Katya had always thought that Mrs. Bee disliked her.

But where was Mrs. Bee taking her? Not to the rear of the house, to Mr. Kidder's studio, but — to the broad front staircase? Up the stairs? Katya protested weakly, "Mrs. Bee, I can't! I can't go upstairs. I've never gone upstairs in this house . . ."

Curtly Mrs. Bee said, "Your portrait has been completed, miss. Master is not painting today but will receive you in his quarters upstairs, as you'd agreed."

"Agreed? When did I . . . agree?"

"Arrangements have been made. Prenuptial documents have been prepared. You will be protected, miss. Master has promised."

Mrs. Bee led Katya up the staircase and into a room with tall narrow windows overlooking the ocean, at a short distance. So blinding was the sunshine in this room that Katya could barely see the ocean, but she'd begun to hear the *slap-slap-slapping* of the surf that was a comforting sound. Briskly Mrs. Bee instructed Katya to remove her clothes — "You can't possibly present yourself to Master in such clothes" — and handed her a shawl in which to wrap herself. Weakly Katya tried to protest, but Mrs. Bee paid no heed, helping her pull off her T-shirt and unhooking her white cotton brassiere; deftly Mrs. Bee loosened Katya's hair and with a gold-backed brush began to brush it vigorously. Katya was mortified by being naked in Mrs. Bee's presence but took comfort in the fact that the shawl was large enough to wrap herself in completely; it appeared to be the identical white cashmere-and-silk shawl that Mr. Kidder had given her when she'd posed nude for him, which Katya had left carelessly behind. That exquisite shawl, which must have been so expensive!

"Come with me now, miss. Master will find you beautiful enough, I am sure."

It was like Mrs. Bee to frown even as she uttered these unexpectedly kind words. Katya blushed in surprise, and with gratitude. Thinking, *All along, Mrs. Bee hasn't hated me? Is this so?*

The housekeeper's hand gripping Katya's was warm but firm.

So spacious and so beautifully furnished was the adjoining room that Katya knew it must be the master bedroom: walls papered in silken ivory with the most minute flecks of gold; a ceiling of elaborately carved white molding; large gilt-framed mirrors; a plush crimson carpet underfoot . . . Against the far wall was an elegantly designed four-poster bed with a canopy of gold and white silk and a carved mahogany headboard like an altarpiece, and in this remarkable bed, which was also a kind of hospital bed to be cranked up like a divan, was Marcus Kidder, lying, or sitting propped up against luxuriant goosefeather pillows. "Katya! My darling! Come to me, dear. I have been waiting, you know." Mr. Kidder smiled wanly at Katya, lifting his arms to her. With a pang Katya saw that Mr. Kidder's skin was waxy-pale and that the injuries to his face — bruises, cuts, rashlike scrapes — had not entirely healed; in the crook of his right forearm you could see a butterfly bandage, indicating that he'd been given IV fluids recently; he appeared to be wearing a white hospital gown, of the kind that ties at the nape of the neck. Yet there was Marcus

Kidder's beautiful snowy-white hair, looking as if it were utterly natural and not a wig; perhaps in fact this was Mr. Kidder's own hair, which had grown miraculously back in since Katya had last seen him. Mr. Kidder's eyes, which were set in shadowy sockets, were yet kindly and intense, and shone with a rapturous sort of hunger that made Katya's heart quicken. Wrapped in the feather-light shawl, barefoot on the crimson carpet, Katya went forward shyly. There was Mrs. Bee at the tall narrow windows, quietly drawing the blinds. Shadows darted from the corners of the room like swift strokes of a charcoal stick. Mrs. Bee was then lighting candles, several intricately designed candelabra fitted with tall cream-colored candles that burned with unusually high tapering flames that gave off a rich perfumed scent that made Katya's head spin.

A door softly closed. Katya glanced around and saw that Mrs. Bee had vanished. On a table beside Mr. Kidder's bed was a silver tray holding two tall bottles of champagne and two champagne glasses and, on a gold-rimmed plate, handfuls of pills, capsules, and tablets. Beneath the perfumed scent of the candles was an astringent medicinal smell.

Slowly, barefoot, Katya went forward to the bed, as Mr. Kidder bade her: "Don't be afraid, my darling! You will not be hurt."

Very subtle was the emphasis on *you*. As Mr. Kidder winked and drew back the brocaded bed cover, so that Katya might slip into the bed beside him, Katya shivered, but she was resolved not to turn back. With some difficulty she climbed up onto and into the large wide bed, which had an unusually hard mattress and was made up with dazzling white linen sheets. Mr. Kidder then gently lowered the cover over Katya, who found herself intimately close beside Mr. Kidder, suddenly so very close that she became short of breath. Mr. Kidder smiled and took Katya's hand. "We must warm you, Katya! Your hand is so cold . . . This is our wedding night, dear, and this will be our honeymoon, this single night. We will celebrate with a champagne toast, yes?"

Now Katya saw that the two tall glasses were filled to the brim with frothy champagne, which Mrs. Bee must have poured before slipping from the room. Gaily Mr. Kidder handed Katya a glass and took a glass for himself; he tapped Katya's glass with his and took a sip of champagne, as Katya did, laughing as minuscule bubbles careened upward into her nose. "Delicious, isn't it! The most delicious champagne I have ever tasted." Katya understood, as Mr. Kidder held out the gold-rimmed plate to her, that she was to feed him the pills, capsules, and tablets, one by one, without haste, placing them on Mr. Kidder's tongue, that he might swallow them down with mouthfuls of champagne. Katya watched, mesmerized. How tempted she was to swallow some of the pills herself! Katya leaned forward and kissed Mr. Kidder's injured face: his forehead, his cheek, his lips, which were unexpectedly warm. Gently Mr. Kidder stroked Katya's hair, and took a strand in his hands to release against his face and against his bared throat. "You must come a little closer, dear. You must be my bride, you know. I will not linger, I promise. I have planned this night for so long, since first seeing you." Katya did not ask when this was, how many years ago. Carefully she took the champagne glass from Mr. Kidder's fingers and lifted it to his mouth, so that he could sip from it even as he was becoming groggy. Liquid ran down his chin; Katya dabbed it away with a tissue. The last of the pills was swallowed, and now came the capsules, and then the tablets. For Katya was Mr. Kidder's bride, but Katya was also Mr. Kidder's nurse. In the Spivak family there were nurses' aides and nurses; when she'd been a little girl, Katya had thought she might become a nurse. It was her task now to replenish the champagne glasses when they were emptied, which Katya did slowly and with care, for she did not want to spill a drop of the precious amber liquid. She had found the champagne taste slightly tart at first but then, by quick degrees, delicious. Of course champagne was delicious. Never had Katya drunk champagne before. There was very little champagne in Vineland, New Jersey.

There could not be a wedding, there could not be a honeymoon, without champagne . . . On a fireplace mantel was a softly ticking clock, and in the near distance the *slap-slap-slapping* of the waves. Close beside the white-haired old man Katya lay, feeling how his breath came now in long tremulous sighs. His eyelids, which were shadowed and bruised, quivered faintly; the icy blue eyes were shut; more and more slowly Mr. Kidder stroked Katya's hair which he'd twined about his throat. "I love you, dear Katya. You are my . . ." The canopied bed seemed to be floating, as if they were borne upon a stream; the crimson carpet had darkened and had become a kind of stream; Katya felt her head spin, the champagne was so intoxicating. Here was a sensation of comfort, warmth. *I belong here, here is my place*, Katya thought. And aloud Katya said, "Here I am, Mr. Kidder. I am here." It was a vow, and a promise. Marcus Kidder would not die an ignoble death. Marcus Kidder would not die except in the arms of his bride. In long shudders his breath came now, in erratic surges, gentle as a sigh, then more labored, then softer, as if fading. As the *slap-slap-slapping* of the surf increased, Mr. Kidder's breathing seemed to lessen. Gusty wind off the Atlantic, wind in the trees above the old shingleboard house, yet you could hear the ocean close behind the house, where the beautiful canopied bed seemed to be headed, floating on the stream. Katya had become sleepy, and lay her head on Mr. Kidder's shoulder, which had little muscle to it, was just an envelope of papery flesh; she felt the bone unexpectedly close beneath, and felt a pang of distress. To warm him, Katya wrapped her long blond hair more firmly around his throat and slipped her arm around his narrow body; she would hold him tight, and snug, as at times, when three-year-old Tricia Engelhardt had been frightened of going to sleep, Katya had done; and Katya held Mr. Kidder's fingers, which were long and thin and were growing cold at the tips, the fingernails turning blue. Just when she believed that Mr. Kidder had lapsed into a deep sleep, he whispered, "Katya? Are you here? With me?

Katya?" and Katya said, squeezing Mr. Kidder in gentle reprimand, "Mr. Kidder, where else would I be?"

Barefoot, Katya was running in the soft sliding sand behind Mr. Kidder's house. Barefoot on the beach, in the direction of the ocean. It was a morning following a storm; the beach was pocked with small glistening puddles and littered with debris — seaweed, sea kelp, the lacerated bodies of fish, quivering jellyfish terrible to see, repulsive, you would not want to step barefoot on a jellyfish's transparent tendrils, for jellyfish washed ashore on the Jersey coast can sting. But Katya Spivak ran leaping, Katya Spivak avoided the stinging tendrils, as she avoided the lacerated bodies of the dead fish, broken shells, and beach grass; her legs were young and strong and muscled; her legs bore her onward, brimming with life; her heart beat with happiness — such strength, suffused with love. For love is strength, there can be no strength without love — Katya would never forget.

Never, never forget. I am the one who loved you, Katya.

Hours later, Katya woke with a start. Her heart beat rapidly, as if, in her sleep, she'd been running, throwing herself against an invisible barrier. She had wanted to follow her companion but had not been able to follow him, and now she could not see where he had gone, she was left behind, stunned. Except for the tall tapering candle flames, this room was dark. Sunshine had vanished behind the drawn blinds. For a sick-sinking moment Katya could not recall where she was. Very still she lay, scarcely daring to breathe as close beside her, so close that her eyes could not take him in, Mr. Kidder lay unmoving; she could not hear him breathe. Stubbornly her slender girl's fingers gripped the old man's fingers, now stiffened with cold.

[165]